# THE GREAT
# SHELBY HOLMES
## MEETS HER MATCH

Also by Elizabeth Eulberg

*The Great Shelby Holmes*

# ⌐•THE GREAT•⌐
# SHELBY HOLMES
## MEETS HER MATCH

## ELIZABETH EULBERG

### illustrated by ERWIN MADRID

BLOOMSBURY
NEW YORK  LONDON  OXFORD  NEW DELHI  SYDNEY

Text copyright © 2017 by Elizabeth Eulberg
Illustrations copyright © 2017 by Erwin Madrid

First published in the United States of America in September 2017
by Bloomsbury Children's Books
www.bloomsbury.com

Bloomsbury is a registered trademark of Bloomsbury Publishing Plc

For information about permission to reproduce selections from this book, write to
Permissions, Bloomsbury Children's Books, 1385 Broadway, New York, New York 10018
Bloomsbury books may be purchased for business or promotional use. For information on
bulk purchases please contact Macmillan Corporate and Premium Sales Department at
specialmarkets@macmillan.com

Library of Congress Cataloging-in-Publication Data
available upon request
ISBN 978-1-68119-054-9 (hardcover) • ISBN 978-1-68119-055-6 (e-book)

Book design by Jessie Gang
Typeset by Westchester Publishing Services
Printed and bound in the U.S.A. by Berryville Graphics Inc., Berryville, Virginia
2 4 6 8 10 9 7 5 3 1

All papers used by Bloomsbury Publishing, Inc., are natural, recyclable products
made from wood grown in well-managed forests. The manufacturing processes
conform to the environmental regulations of the country of origin.

*For my extraordinary editor, Catherine Onder,*
*who has made Watson, Shelby,*
*and this writer better with each book*

# THE GREAT
# SHELBY HOLMES
## MEETS HER MATCH

# ↶·CHAPTER·↷
# 1

You'd think having a friend who's a know-it-all would be annoying. And okay, at times it really, really is. *But* it can also be fascinating. And extremely helpful.

Especially if it's your first day at a new school.

"I see Sasha's parents didn't take her to Greece like they promised," Shelby remarked as we walked down the hallway at the Harlem Academy of the Arts. I followed her gaze to a white girl with her blond hair in a ponytail. There was absolutely nothing about this girl that would've led a normal person to think that Sasha didn't go on some family vacation.

But while Shelby Holmes was many things, normal wasn't one of them.

"How did you—" I began to ask before she cut me off.

"Like it isn't obvious," she replied with a huff.

A teacher standing outside a classroom looked up from a

folder. As soon as he saw Shelby, he quickly turned around, went into his classroom, and closed the door.

The only thing that seemed obvious to me was that there was a path being cleared for Shelby as we walked. I'd learned a few things from Shelby in the three weeks I'd known her. One was to make deductions based on people's behavior. Right now, I was deducing that nobody in the school wanted Shelby to do that thing she did.

Me included.

I also learned to listen to everything she says. And that she's always right.

While she kept casually spilling the secrets of our class-mates and teachers as we continued down the hall, I looked around my new school. From the outside, it looked like a standard school building: redbrick and nothing special. But as soon as we stepped inside, it was everything I'd hoped a charter school focused on the arts would be: the walls were covered with student artwork, music filled the halls, and there were tryout flyers up for the fall musical. There was even an entire glass display case filled with books. But they weren't regular books found in other schools. These were the yearly anthologies the Academy put out featuring the best student writing.

*Someday I'll be in there*, I hoped.

Yeah, I could totally get used to a place like this. I had

two classes where I got to focus on my writing. *Two! And* I was going to be staying here. No more moving for the Watsons. We were making New York City our home.

Of course that meant I really needed to make a good first impression, since I'd be sticking around. I was used to being the new kid. I mean, I'd spent all eleven years of my life moving from army post to army post. But this was my last day as the new kid at a new place. It was different.

Shelby grunted, which brought me back to her orientation of my new classmates. "Like it isn't abundantly apparent she got kicked out of camp this summer."

"Who are you talking about?" I glanced around the hallway.

"Watson," Shelby said with a disapproving shake of her head. "What have I been telling you about observing?"

"I have been observing, but it would help if you could tell me *how* you know these things. Or, you know, start with *who* you're even talking about." My eyes swept my fellow classmates to find a clue about anything having to do with *anyone* at this point. I kept observing the same things as Shelby, but could never see what she saw.

"Fine!" she said with a groan. Her hand flew up and pointed to three girls talking by a locker. "Do you see how two of the girls have matching homemade rope bracelets? Standard last-day-of-camp fare. Pretty uninspiring if you ask me. Charlotte's not only missing one, but notice the lack of color on her, unlike the other two."

Yeah, the two other girls were more tan or whatever, but that could mean anything. How on earth did Shelby come up with someone being kicked out of camp?

Okay, I technically know how she did it. By deductive reasoning. But that doesn't mean I fully understood it. What Shelby's been trying to teach me to do is to assemble a list of likely scenarios based on observations, and then decide which option fit best. In the case of these three girls, the only scenario I had was that just one of them used sunscreen.

Shelby took my silence as ignorance. "I had to listen to them blather on and on last year about their horseback riding camp. So the missing markers of attending said camp for an extended period were glaringly obvious on Charlotte."

But I wasn't here last year, so how could *I* have known?

"And no, you're not off the hook simply because you weren't here last year," Shelby said as if she had read my mind. Maybe she had. "What can you tell by their interaction? Look closely," she instructed me.

I studied the three girls. Hmmm . . . Now that Shelby pointed it out, the two tan girls were talking animatedly, moving around their hands, laughing and talking over each other. While the other girl shifted uncomfortably from foot to foot, giving a polite smile every once in a while. So she didn't know the story the others were telling. And appeared a little jealous of it.

Maybe Shelby was right. (Wait, there's no maybe. She *was* right.)

"Okay, one girl feels left out, but still . . ." I could only see things once Shelby pointed them out. It was hard for me to put two and two together with basically nothing.

Shelby continued to walk down the hallway, while I tried to come up with more deductions.

"Maybe she has an allergy and couldn't go?" I took a stab in the dark.

"She went the previous year. It was all she talked about at the beginning of fifth grade."

"Oh, so you're friends."

Shelby stopped and looked at me with her patented look of disgust and aggravation. It was a look I'd gotten used to pretty quickly. "Friends? Oh, please be serious, Watson."

I knew Shelby didn't really think friends were important, but was it such a ridiculous assumption? Shelby was familiar enough with this Charlotte person to know she went to camp every summer. That would've required a conversation, wouldn't it? Some friendly banter? She couldn't decipher everything about a person by simply observing.

"Freak!" someone shouted in the hallway to the snickers of a few students.

On the other hand . . . maybe Shelby really didn't have friends, since everybody at this school was aware of what she could do—most of her clients were her classmates—and seemed to want no part of her.

I don't know. I just assumed everybody at school would think that she was weird (because she was) but still be impressed by her. I'll admit that I thought she was just a freaky science geek when we met on my first day in our new apartment building. But once I got past her grumpy attitude, I respected her. Everybody in our Harlem neighborhood admires her for her abilities.

But instead, when Shelby walked by, shoulders tensed and voices lowered.

It didn't take a genius of Shelby's caliber to realize that she wasn't well liked at school.

And here I was, on my first day, walking down the hallway with her. So much for a great start.

*Stop it, John.* I reminded myself that Shelby had helped me a lot during my first few days in New York City. We were friends. (Okay, she was my *only* friend here.) Plus, we were partners.

Shelby stopped dead in her tracks to the unease of the students around us. She was staring at a teacher who was in the hallway greeting students.

"The new science teacher, Mr. Crosby," Shelby informed me, but there was an edge to her voice.

I ignored the stares from the kids around us as I waited for her to tell me about our teacher.

Shelby remained quiet, her eyes surveying Mr. Crosby. My guess was that she was building up tension, something she liked to do, for a dramatic reveal.

"Well?" I asked her, anxious to get to my first class.

Then Shelby Holmes, detective extraordinaire, said the three words I thought would never come out of her mouth.

"I don't know."

# ~CHAPTER~
# 2

I'M NOT SURE WHAT WORRIED ME MORE: THAT THERE WAS something the great Shelby Holmes didn't know, or that she marched right up to the new teacher and dropped to the floor to start examining him from the shoes up.

"Excuse me?" Mr. Crosby asked the top of Shelby's red frizzy curls. "Can I help you with something?"

When Shelby didn't answer, Mr. Crosby looked at me.

Since this poor teacher was new, I guessed somebody needed to tell him that Shelby was just being . . . well, Shelby.

And that lucky person was me.

"Hi," I said with a friendly smile. "I'm John Watson. It's my first day here, too."

"Hello, John," Mr. Crosby replied as he moved his feet around in an effort to shake Shelby. Of course this only resulted in irritating her. "Nice to meet you."

"You, too. I just moved to the neighborhood from Maryland, near DC. My mom used to work in the military.

Now she's a doctor over at the Columbia University Medical Center." I don't know why I felt the need to give Mr. Crosby my life story, but I was trying to put him at ease while Shelby did her thing.

In the short time we'd been working together, this had become my role in our partnership. Although it had taken a while for Shelby to realize that she needed my help. She definitely had the smarts to solve cases on her own, but it was her people skills that needed some work.

"Yeah, this is—"

"Shelby Holmes," Mr. Crosby finished my sentence. "Yes, I've been . . . informed." I was pretty sure he'd been *warned*, but caught himself.

I attempted to do my own investigation of Mr. Crosby. He looked like your typical white guy teacher: blue button-down shirt, khaki pants, and brown loafers. He was probably in his late twenties. He had short brown hair, brown eyes, and an average height and build. Pretty standard. Nothing remarkable about him.

Maybe not everybody had some story that Shelby could decode by a smudge on their glasses or how they tied their shoes.

Could it be possible that Mr. Crosby was simply a regular, boring teacher?

Shelby finally stood up and narrowed her eyes at him.

"Hello, Shelby," Mr. Crosby said with a hesitant smile. "Did you find whatever you're looking for?"

Shelby's scowl confirmed that she, in fact, had not. "You taught at a private school before? No!" she screeched. "Don't tell me!"

Mr. Crosby's attention shifted again to me. "Why don't I make this easy for everybody: I taught at Miss Adler's School for Girls on the Upper East Side for—"

"Two years," Shelby interrupted him. "Yes, I'm not an imbecile."

Mr. Crosby's eyes grew wide. "How did you . . ."

Apparently he didn't take those warnings about Shelby seriously.

"It's just this thing she does." I repeated the line that I'd been told when I had first met Shelby. It was something I'd been forced to say a lot these last three weeks.

My attention drifted to a familiar face in the hallway. It took me a second to remember that I already knew one other person who goes to the Academy.

"Tamra!" I called out.

Tamra Lacy was walking down the hall with three other girls. Even though she had on the same maroon Harlem Academy of the Arts polo shirt that every student wore, it was clear from her appearance that Tamra had money. I mean, yeah, I already knew that from being at her family's insane mega-apartment that overlooked Central Park. (And having met her family's personal chef and maid and driver.) But it was more than that. It was the way her black patent leather shoes shone in contrast to the other girls' canvas shoes, and how neatly pressed her shirt was compared to the wrinkles the majority of us sported.

Maybe my deductive reasoning wasn't so shabby after all.

Yet there was one mystery I couldn't figure out: why Tamra didn't seem to hear me.

"Tamra!" I called out again. "Hey!"

Her dark brown eyes glanced sideways. "Hi, John," she said softly, almost like she was embarrassed. A couple of her friends were whispering while stealing glances at Shelby.

*Interesting.* Well, it wasn't interesting that Tamra's friends would treat Shelby like everybody else did. What didn't make sense was why Tamra was being so cold to us, especially since it was Shelby who found Tamra's missing dog.

Although Tamra wasn't the first Lacy to disappoint me. It turned out it was her brother Zane, the first (and so far only) non-Shelby friend I made in New York, who stole her dog. Not surprisingly, after I helped Shelby prove he was the culprit, Zane didn't want to be friends with me anymore.

"Excuse me, John?" Mr. Crosby was leaning against the wall, Shelby's eyes only inches from his shirt. "Do you think you could help me? It's about time you get to class."

"Oh, right!" I took Shelby's arm and led her away, despite her protests.

"Something's not right," Shelby said between clenched teeth.

"Or maybe he's just a regular dude. Not everybody's a criminal mastermind." I took out my schedule and double-checked what room I was going to.

"Next door on the left," Shelby remarked. "I'll be across the hall if you need me."

"Thanks! Have a good day, Shelby!" I went to open the classroom door, but found it was locked.

"Your other left, Watson," Shelby said with a grimace. "And one more thing."

I stopped, waiting for some words of wisdom from Shelby that would help me navigate this school, just like she had helped me get around my new neighborhood. Although school was where I could really shine: I was a decent student. I could make friends easily.

But Shelby was Shelby, and I'd take any advice from her I could get.

"There's something that teacher is hiding. Mark my words: I'm going to find out what."

Shelby's face was deadly serious.

# CHAPTER 3

I GUESS THE FIRST DAY OF SCHOOL IS PRETTY MUCH THE SAME everywhere, even in New York City.

The morning was the basic blur of being introduced to teachers, getting a rundown of the upcoming semester, and meeting a ton of new kids. And I was called to the nurse's office so she could talk to me about my diabetes. All standard first-day fare.

Being the new kid wasn't too bad. It was a role I was familiar with. My army-post background definitely made me stick out, but in a good way. Even though Shelby had given me the nickname Watson, since there were two other Johns in our grade, most people had started to refer to me as "Army Dude." Hey, I'd take it.

However, as I walked to lunch, my least favorite first-day feeling came over me: the fear in the pit in my stomach that nobody would want to sit with me. I had no idea if Shelby and I had the same lunch period. I hadn't seen her since classes started.

"Hey, Army Dude!" John Wu (aka John #1 and the only John referred to by his first name) called out to me as I walked into the cafeteria, tightly gripping my lunch bag. "Come join us!" John and three other guys made room for me at their table.

"Thanks!" I said gratefully as I sat with them. Since our school focused on the arts, students often introduced themselves not only by name, but by what arts program they were in. John Wu was in acting, Bryant (aka John #2, who, like me, goes by his last name) was in music, Carlos was in art, and Jason was in writing with me.

"What did you think of writing class?" Jason asked as he pulled his long dreads into a ponytail.

"It was cool." Ever since Mom told me about the school, I couldn't wait to be in a creative writing class. Our teacher, Ms. Onder, had already given us our first

writing assignment: every day we were supposed to write in a journal. It could be traditional journal writing or total fiction. We just had to write every day. "I've always loved English class, but to have a class all about writing is the best. I hope I can keep up."

"Yeah. Sometimes the words won't flow, you know?"

I did know. I used to write stories all the time, but then my parents broke up and I didn't really have the motivation. But now . . . I don't know. While it still stung not to have Dad around, my writing had picked up again thanks to Shelby. I'd started to record our adventures in a journal, which was perfect for Ms. Onder's class. While I only reported the truth when it came to Shelby, I wondered if people would believe what she could do. She was pretty unbelievable.

"I hear ya," Carlos agreed. "Some days I don't have that spark to paint. Although when we do our section on modern art, I could rub a booger on a canvas and it'd be considered art."

"Dude, I'm trying to eat," John Wu said.

"See, John, you acting guys have it easy," Jason replied as he bit into an apple. "You simply recite whatever we writers write. Army Dude and I are the real creators, right?"

I bobbed my head as Jason continued to tell everybody how writers ruled. Although I had never really thought about it like that. I just had stories I wanted to tell. Things I wanted to share. Mostly I wanted to tell my story. So much was happening to me, and writing helped me remember every single detail. This lunch with my new friends was just the beginning.

I knew it had only been three hours, but I loved this school. Yeah, the basics were still the same, but it was somehow so different being around other creative people. I pictured us talking about art and reading and life. It was almost like I was a grown-up.

Bryant flipped his shaggy blond hair that covered most of his pale face. "At least you guys are excited for your classes. We were handed a new piece in music this morning, and I'll give you one guess who nailed it on the first try."

They all laughed at some inside joke.

"I mean, at least you have a chance to be the top person in your department," Bryant complained.

"What instrument do you play?" I asked as he picked at his sandwich.

"Violin. I was always the best until *she* came along."

I followed Bryant's glare to Shelby, who was sitting alone at a table in the middle of the cafeteria. She was reading an extremely large chemistry book as she shoved an entire cookie into her mouth.

Shelby was *that* good at the violin?

I didn't know why that surprised me. Shelby was good at everything. Well, except for sports. And I'm not only talking about playing sports. Shelby knew nothing about sports. *Nothing.* She didn't feel that kind of information should take up "precious real estate" in her brain attic.

Bryant groaned. "I could handle being second best if she wasn't so smug about it."

Sure sounded like Shelby.

Carlos hit Jason on the shoulder. "Army Dude doesn't know about Harlem Academy's very own supersleuth. Watch out for her, man. She can figure out your whole life story in four point five seconds."

"Just stay away from her, period," Bryant warned me as he took a big bite of his sandwich.

"Come on, guys, she's not that bad," Jason came to Shelby's defense while I remained mute on the subject. "We're all freaks of some kind, right? I mean, Bryant, you're an eleven-year-old violin prodigy. How much more geeky can you get? John over there can spew Shakespeare from memory."

John Wu pushed up his wire-rimmed glasses and reached his arm out. " 'Be not afraid of greatness: some are born great, some achieve greatness, and some have greatness thrust upon them.' "

"Yep, right there! *Exactly*!" Jason nodded at John Wu.

"And Carlos, you're always covered in ink doodles or paint. As for me, I'm always paying attention to what you say so I can steal it and portray y'all poorly in a work of fiction." Jason let out a huge laugh, which was contagious, and we all began laughing with him. Except for Bryant.

"Yeah, yeah. Easy for you to say," Bryant grumbled. His face was getting red. "She's not in your program."

"She's in an acting class with me," John replied.

"Yeah, well, you're just defending her because you hired her last year," Bryant argued.

John shrugged. "She found the script for the play with all my notes. Totally worth the sack of candy. Admit it, you'd go to her if you lost your violin."

That seemed to quiet Bryant for a bit.

I looked over at Shelby, whose face was hidden in her book. I remembered when Tamra told Shelby about her dog; Shelby said she was someone people came to if they needed something. Even then I felt bad that she was used by her fellow classmates like that, but she didn't seem to care. Funny thing was that I did.

"Shelby's my neighbor," I confessed. I wanted them to realize that she was someone beyond a supersleuth. "We live in the same building. And . . . we're friends."

They all stopped chewing their food and looked at me.

"Hold on." Carlos started laughing like I'd just told a

joke. "You mean she has friends? Like, you guys hang out and do normal friend things?"

*Define* normal?

"Well, I mean, I help her with her cases sometimes."

"Help her *how*?" Bryant narrowed his eyes. "Is there anything she doesn't know? Look at her!" He gestured to Shelby. "What sixth grader reads a giant chemistry book for *fun*!"

I didn't want to remind them that Shelby should technically be in fourth grade since she'd skipped a couple grades. I turned to make sure Shelby couldn't hear us. Even though she was four tables away and reading a book, I couldn't help but feel like she was watching me. "She's simply putting facts away in her brain attic."

"Brain attic?" John and Carlos asked in unison.

"I know, I know," I said. "It's how she stores away information to help her solve cases. She's really smart."

"I guess that's one way you could describe her," Carlos said with a snicker.

Jason let out a huge groan. "Aw man, you are going to have way better things to write about if you're working with her. Don't go making me look boring." Then he did his contagious laugh again.

I instantly knew that Jason and I would be good friends. He's a writer like me and seemed to get that being friends with Shelby was anything but dull.

"Okay, okay," Carlos said as he looked nervously at Shelby. He hunched over and said in a near whisper, "So, like, did she really stop a bank from being robbed with a paper clip and fork?"

He was joking, right?

John shook his head. "No way. That can't be true. Right, Army Dude? Also, the mayor does *not* call her every morning for a security briefing." His face fell as he leaned in. "Does he?"

I could only stare back at them, waiting for a punch line that never came.

It appeared as if the exploits of one Shelby Holmes had been greatly exaggerated.

Jason laughed. "Don't listen to these fools, John Watson. They'll believe anything."

Carlos began to protest, but Jason waved him off. "Yeah, yeah, you don't believe any of it, but you'll go a different way to class to avoid running into her."

"She once knew that I hadn't finished my homework the second I walked into class," Carlos said. "It was freaky. I had planned some excuse, but she outed me in front of everyone. How did she know?"

Body language was my guess. Shelby had been showing me that the way people hold themselves could tell a lot about them. Like this morning with the girl who wasn't at camp. Right now, observing the guys, they seemed to be scared of what Shelby could do, which was understandable. But I also sensed they had a begrudging respect for her.

"Well," I said as I got up with my empty lunch bag. "All I'll say is that I've seen some crazy stuff since hanging with her. And she's actually pretty cool."

It felt good to stand up for Shelby. She'd done so much for me, it was the least I could do for her. Yeah, it was freaky what she could do, but she wasn't *that* bad.

As the warning bell sounded, I made my way to my locker. I couldn't help but laugh. Here I'd thought people wouldn't believe my stories about Shelby, but it seemed the myth might be bigger than the actual Shelby.

Shelby was waiting for me at my locker.

"Hey, Shelby!" I said loudly.

An amused smile spread on Shelby's face. *"Actually pretty cool*? Really, Watson? People might start talking." She shook her head before turning on her heel and walking away.

Of course she had heard everything. *Of course* she did.

# CHAPTER 4

"SOUNDS LIKE YOU HAD A GOOD FIRST DAY OF SCHOOL."

"Yeah, it was pretty good, Dad."

Yep. *STOP THE PRESSES!* I was talking to my dad.

He'd kind of disappeared my first week here. He didn't call when he said he would, and then he wouldn't answer my calls. It was really frustrating. And it hurt. Like, a lot.

Things had gotten a little better over the past two weeks. It wasn't perfect. If there was a perfect version of my life, he'd be here. But hey, at least we were talking.

"I'm really proud of you, son," he replied. His voice sounded closer than the thousand miles that separated New York City and our old army post in Kentucky where he worked in the recruiting department. "Why don't we video chat next time so I can see your face. You sound older. I hope you aren't growing up too fast without your old man around."

The thing was, so much has happened since I got here, I did feel older. Maybe it was because it was just Mom and me, or maybe it was solving cases with Shelby. People relied on me more now than they did on the post.

"Tell your mother I said hello," he added a bit cautiously.

"I will," I replied, knowing that she'd at least be happy he called when he said he would. This time.

There was a knock on our door, and since there was only one person who ever came to visit me, I knew who it was.

I opened the door, and Shelby took one quick look at me. "And how is your father?"

Normally, I'd be impressed with Shelby's ability to pluck information seemingly out of thin air, but with the stupid grin on my face, it would've been obvious to anybody that I just talked to my dad.

I missed him. Sometimes talking to him made me miss him more, but that twenty-minute conversation about my first day of school made me feel like he was part of my life again.

"What's going on?" I asked Shelby as she plunked down on the couch. "Did you have a good day?"

I hadn't seen Shelby that much today. We only had one class together, science. Then she left class quickly, and I couldn't find her once school was over.

"I survived."

"Where'd you go off to after school?"

"I had things to do."

"Oh." I was a little disappointed that she hadn't included me in whatever she was doing, since "things" with Shelby usually meant there was a case.

"Hey," I said, trying to sound casual. "You want to join me for lunch tomorrow?" I felt bad that she was sitting by herself at lunch, and I wanted her to join the guys and me. I mean, I know she didn't *need* friends. But who wants to eat lunch by themselves?

She grimaced. "Why would I want to waste precious research time?"

"You know . . . to make some friends."

"I have enough friends." She gestured at me. By the look on her face, it appeared that one might be too many.

"Well, maybe it would make things easier for you," I reasoned. It would make people see that she was kinda cool, even with her caustic attitude. Though of course I didn't say that.

"Please, Watson, school's easy enough."

Usually I'd agree with her, but it didn't seem like the Harlem Academy of the Arts was going to be easy. I already had so much homework for every class. Who gave homework on the first day?

I gestured at the pile of books in front of us on the coffee table. "Please tell me this much homework isn't normal."

Shelby shrugged. "I suppose one could consider the

mundane tasks assigned as *work*. I finished mine before we even left school."

"What?" How was that possible? "Science, too?"

"I had that done before Mr. Crosby could even figure out what he was assigning us."

I'd sneaked a few glances at Shelby during class. She sat front and center and had her head down, scribbling in her notebook the entire time. I thought she was writing down everything Crosby was saying, not finishing her homework.

"I also had enough time to start my investigation," she added casually, although I could tell she wanted me to ask her about it.

"We have a case?"

"Potentially. I started doing preliminary research on my suspect during class."

There was a suspect in science class?

Then it hit me.

I slapped my hand against my forehead. "This isn't about Mr. Crosby, is it?"

Shelby pointed her finger at me. "There's something off about him. He looks at me in a weird way."

*WHO DOESN'T?* I wanted to ask, but I bit my tongue. But *seriously*? I'd seen nothing but weird looks for Shelby from kids *and* teachers today.

"Hold on." I narrowed my eyes at her. "What exactly were you doing after school?"

Her eyes darted sideways.

Oh, she was so busted.

"Please tell me you weren't stalking our new teacher."

"It's called tailing a person of interest," she replied with a sniff.

"Well, did you find anything?" I asked, although I knew she hadn't. If she had anything on Crosby, she would've marched into the apartment with that told-ya-so grin she so loves.

"It's still too early to have a fully formed case against him."

"Shelby . . ." I wanted to reason with her, but already knew I was in a losing battle.

"Fine, don't believe me."

It was hard to not believe Shelby since she was, say it with me, *always right*. But maybe, just maybe she was wrong this one time.

"Okay, okay," I said to appease her. I knew Shelby's suspicions weren't simply going to vanish. Neither was the towering pile of books in front of me. "I really need to get to my homework," I said as I picked up one of my books. I didn't even know where to start. Usually I would always do my English homework first, and as much as I was itching to write about my first day of school, I knew that would be easy compared to my math homework. And science. And history.

"I can't believe you're already done," I said. "It's so much."

Shelby looked up at the ceiling and tilted her head. "You're right. All this homework is extremely overwhelming, to be honest with you."

*Aha! It wasn't only me!*

"Do you want to study together?" I offered.

She wrung her hands in her lap. "Truthfully, there's a chance I may need to drop down to fifth-grade science."

I was stunned. It was hard to believe.

*Wait a second.* Not only had Shelby said she'd already finished our homework, but now she wouldn't look me in the eyes. Her fidgeting hands were a clue that she was uneasy. She twice reiterated that she was telling the truth or being honest, pushing that point a little too hard. Shelby always told me to observe, and what I was observing was that Shelby Holmes wasn't telling the truth. And I was going to call her on it.

"Why are you lying?"

Shelby dropped her hands by her side. "Well done, Watson! Which nonverbal clue tipped you off the most?"

"Wait. You were testing me?"

"Yes! And you did splendidly." Shelby patted me on the back. "Now for your next assignment, I'm going to—"

I cut her off. "Shelby, I have a ton of homework. Can this wait?"

"Do you think criminals wait?" she countered. "There's

so much you have yet to learn. While you've improved in observing, there are still many elements you need to master to truly be helpful: chromatography, fingerprinting, entomology, dental forensics, lab testing—"

"Fingerprinting? Lab testing?" I asked since those were the only things I'd even heard of. "Have you even had to use that stuff?"

"A good detective is always up-to-date with the latest investigation techniques." Shelby flipped open one of my notebooks. "How are your art skills? Judging by your penmanship, I presume they're average."

"Hey!" I said as I grabbed the notebook out of her hand. My handwriting wasn't that bad. Shelby's was the worst— she wrote so quickly it was nearly impossible to read. "I'm okay at drawing, I guess. Why?"

"It's helpful to sketch crime scenes and suspects."

"Then why have I never once seen you sketch anything?"

"I don't need to." She tapped her head. "Everything I need is in here."

Of course it was. As much as I appreciated that Shelby was willing to teach me more about solving cases, it would have to wait. If I didn't get my schoolwork done, I was going to be in big trouble. Shelby Holmes could be intimidating, but she had nothing on my mom when she got angry.

"How about this weekend?" I offered.

"I suppose so." Shelby slumped on the couch, her feet inches from the ground. "I'll come up with something fun."

*Uh-oh.* Shelby and I had very different ideas of what was considered fun.

She finally got up, an extra bounce in her step. "Maybe I'll call in some favors and see if I can get access to a cadaver."

"Wait!" I called out to her. "Please, no dead body parts. Promise me."

(Like I should have to ever say those words to anybody. EVER.)

"But it would be—"

"*Promise,*" I urged her.

"Fine, I promise." She grimaced. "Sometimes you're no fun, Watson."

See what I meant? Very different definitions. Very.

# ~ CHAPTER ~
## 5

JUST LAST MONTH, I COULDN'T WAIT FOR SCHOOL TO BEGIN. Now that I finished my second week of school, I longed for the lazy days of summer. (Although *lazy* was not a word you could use to describe anything Shelby Holmes–related.)

I was busy. Crazy busy. There was homework. There were writing assignments. There were chores at home. And more homework. And, you know, making time for new friends.

And then there were my lessons from Shelby.

"Be careful," she instructed me as I placed a casting

frame around a footprint in the wet soil of Mrs. Hudson's garden. "You have the benefit of casting a much larger print than I did when I had to find out who was destroying Mrs. Hudson's kale. My eyes told me it was a rabbit, but I needed a cast to confirm."

The footprint cast was going to dry overnight. Then tomorrow I was supposed to tell Shelby about the person who left it (although I already knew it was her). She had taught me all about tread patterns, foot measurements, and gaits.

"Of course, then I had to figure out where the rabbit came from," Shelby continued, as she often did, bragging about her old cases. "That led me to not only capture the animal, but also to return it to its owners down the street. Two cases solved with one helpful technique."

"That's really impressive, Shelby."

While it was, in fact, impressive, I was really just buttering Shelby up.

In creative writing class, Ms. Onder suggested we start putting our work up online to gain an audience and get feedback from readers. I wanted to start an online journal about our adventures, but I needed Shelby's permission.

Part of me assumed she'd want me to do it since it would feed her ego to get credit for all the work she'd done around our neighborhood and school. But there was another part that was worried she would find it silly. She always saw me writing on the stoop and knew about my journal, but she never asked me about it.

Maybe because she already knew what was in it. Or maybe because she didn't care.

"Hey, Shelby." I tried to sound natural as I mixed the plaster of paris to pour into the imprint. "You know that journal I've been keeping about our cases?"

"Yes," she replied as she stuck her face down near the soil, inspecting my work.

"Would you mind if I put it online? It's for class." I could hardly contain my nerves. I could always change names and details if she said no, but I really wanted to report the truth.

Okay, and I'll admit that I hoped there'd be enough people in school who would be curious about Shelby that I'd be guaranteed some readers. Jason was always snatching my notebook to read the latest entry. The only problem was, I was running out of things to say. We hadn't had a case since school started.

"Do whatever." Shelby stood up and wiped her hands on her jeans.

*Really?* That was it? I didn't think she'd make it so easy. She never made things easy. (See: being on my hands and knees mixing plaster in our backyard on a sunny Saturday afternoon.)

"Why do you look surprised?" she called me out.

"Oh, nothing, I just . . . You're sure?"

She scowled at me. "Of course I'm sure. Would you like me to retract my answer?"

"No!"

Shelby sighed. "Here's another lesson for you, Watson: Never give someone the opportunity to reverse their decision if you already have the answer you want."

"Yeah, no, yeah," I stammered.

"Are you okay here?"

"I think so."

"Okay, good. I have a pressing matter that I need to attend to upstairs. Please come up when you've completed your task."

"What pressing matter?" I asked.

Her reply was to walk away. (Again, she never makes things easy.)

I kept my eyes glued on the plaster of paris to make sure I mixed it to the right consistency. Shelby said it had to be like pancake batter, which only made me hungry. Once I thought I had it, I slowly poured the mixture into the shoe impression.

A loud bang came from the building, like something heavy dropped on the floor. The sound actually made me smile since it reminded me of the first time I met Shelby. She had set off an explosion upstairs during a science experiment gone wrong. Then my smile disappeared as I had a horrible feeling that whatever that noise was had to do with my next assignment.

I finished with the cast, then made my way up to Shelby's apartment. It was eerily quiet. When I got to the landing in front of 221B, the door was slightly ajar.

"Shelby?"

I hesitated before stepping inside. It felt weird to just go into someone's home, but Shelby knew I was coming up here and probably left it unlocked for me.

As soon as I walked into the living room, I knew something was wrong. One of the armchairs had been knocked on its side. I went over to look at it and let out a scream.

"*AHHHHHHHHHHHHHHHHHHHH!!!!!!*"

There, on the other side of the chair, was Shelby, covered in blood. Her eyes were closed.

Sir Arthur started barking upstairs. It took me a second to form words. But as soon as I found my voice, I began shouting, "MRS. HUDSON! ANYBODY! SOMEBODY! CALL 9-1-1!"

Shelby opened her eyes, and I let out another scream. "Seriously, Watson?" she said with a sneer. "How reassuring that you remain so cool and poised under pressure."

"Wh—wha—" I stuttered, my entire body shaking.

"And you've upset Sir Arthur."

Shelby was concerned about *her dog* being upset? WHAT ABOUT ME?

"What on earth is going on?" Mrs. Hudson called out as she climbed the stairs.

Shelby groaned. "Great, you've also managed to interfere with a crime scene." She sat up and began shouting, "Everything's fine, Mrs. Hudson. Watson just decided to up the hysterics this afternoon." She rolled her eyes.

"Oh, okay!" Mrs. Hudson replied, and her footsteps receded. I don't think she would've been that calm if she saw the state of the apartment. Or Shelby, for that matter.

I took a deep breath. "What. Is. Going. On?"

Shelby wiped away some blood that was trickling down her face. "I've given you a case to investigate. You're welcome, by the way. Unfortunately, one of the clues has been mucked up by your improper handling of a crime scene, but there should still be sufficient evidence to continue. So tell me, what have you observed?"

"WHAT HAVE I OBSERVED?" My voice was shrill. "Are you INSANE? I thought you were dead!" My pulse was racing. I don't think I'd ever been so freaked out in my entire life.

"That's precisely what you're supposed to think since my murder is the case you're trying to solve. However, you've only managed to prove to be more a lover of the dramatic arts than a detective, with all your ranting."

"SHELBY!" I yelled at her. "I think I'M going to be the one to kill you!"

"Please be serious, Watson."

Oh, I was being serious. My entire body was still shaking from nerves. And shock. Definitely shock.

"This training exercise took a lot of time to set up, and I would appreciate it if you'd give it a try," Shelby said, irritation in her voice. Like *I* was the one being unreasonable.

"We're never going to be called in to investigate a murder," I reasoned.

"There's always hope," Shelby replied with a wistful look on her face.

This was unbelievable. Truly unbelievable. The shock was wearing off, and now all I felt was anger. "You want to know what I see?" I asked.

"Not see, Watson. *Observe*," she corrected me.

"I *see* a completely delusional person!" I started looking around the room, then stopped. I wasn't going to give her the pleasure of finding her clues. There was no way I was going to encourage her. I already knew that I was going to be opening doors around here with a lot more caution. Who knew what other surprises she had planned for me.

"Ugh!" Shelby fell back on the floor. "I *would* kill for a case like this. I'm so bored," she whined.

So Shelby was bored and decided to stage a murder.

We really needed a new case.

# CHAPTER 6

"AT LONG LAST, YOU HAVE A CASE," SHELBY SAID TO ME AT her locker the following Wednesday.

"Really?" I asked. After I refused to talk to her for a day after the "murder" fiasco, Shelby promised me no more fake blood (I'd been assured it was a mixture of corn syrup, red dye, and flour), and I'd forgiven her for nearly giving me a heart attack. "We have a case?"

"No. *You* have a case," Shelby replied. "Let's face it, you need the practice."

I ignored Shelby's dig and instead got excited. My very own case! And Shelby trusted me to figure it out on my own.

*Come on Watson, you can do this.*

"Watson, this is Tanya, a fourth grader in the music program." She gestured toward a little white girl with pigtails. Then Shelby held up a piggy bank. "This is Tanya's bank, which has been losing funds continuously over the past two weeks. A few coins disappear each day."

Shelby studied the ceramic pig from every angle, even smelling it. Shelby had been harping about how investigating involved all five senses. Guess she was trying them all out on this case, although she hadn't licked it. Yet.

She smiled as she handed it to me. "This one is a piece of cake, even for you."

I took the bank in my hands and copied what Shelby had done.

I had nothing.

*Think, Watson.*

"It was a family member," I ventured a guess. Who else would have access to Tanya's piggy bank? Unless it was a babysitter. Or someone who worked for the family. But would they waste time taking a few coins here and there?

I glanced at Shelby, whose expression remained blank. She wasn't going to give me any hints.

"Not a family member?" I fished for a clue.

Shelby snatched the bank from my hands. "It was your younger sibling," she declared to Tanya.

"What? How?" Tanya asked. (I had the exact same questions.)

Shelby sighed as she flipped over the ceramic pig. "First, do you see the dark stain near the cork?"

Tanya held up the bank closely to her eyes. "I guess . . ."

We both looked at Shelby expectantly, but her attention was now across the hallway. I followed her gaze to Mr. Crosby, who was headed our way and talking to Principal Loh. Shelby narrowed her eyes suspiciously. Both Crosby and Principal Loh glanced at Shelby and stopped talking when they walked past us.

Okay, that *was* weird. Although most people froze when they were within eavesdropping distance of Shelby.

"You can't still be on that," I said to Shelby. During our science classes with Crosby, Shelby continued to sit in the front row and take notes the entire time. But I thought at this point she was actually, you know, taking notes for class.

"What?" Tanya looked around the hall. "What about my piggy bank?"

Once Mr. Crosby and Principal Loh turned the corner and disappeared from view, Shelby snapped her attention back to us.

"Smell it," she demanded, pointing toward the dark spot by the cork.

Tanya took a step away from the piggy bank.

"Smell it," Shelby repeated slowly as if she were talking to a small child.

I didn't smell anything when I gave the bank a sniff.

Tanya did as Shelby instructed. "Is that . . . ?"

"Yes, it's chocolate," Shelby stated.

*Seriously*? *Tanya* smelled something? I mean, if Shelby would've told *me* exactly where to smell, I would've figured it out. At least I hoped I would have. But then again, what did the chocolate even mean?

"Organic dark chocolate, to be precise," Shelby said with a twitch of her nose. "I much prefer the taste of milk chocolate myself. And before you inquire how I knew you had a sibling, I'll save you the trouble. You have all the markings of an older sibling: wrinkled clothing, especially around the quadriceps where the sibling no doubt hangs onto your legs. In addition to your messy appearance, your lunches, if you ever bring one to school, are packed haphazardly at best. I once observed that a pacifier was accidentally packed in your lunch in lieu of a juice box. Clear signs of neglect due to your parents' paying attention to a significantly younger child. A sibling whose hands need to be cleaned with more regularity, evidently. You no doubt queried said sibling about your piggy bank?"

"Yeah, but Katie's not even two. She can hardly string a sentence together. She kept saying no, and honestly I didn't think she could even figure out how to open it."

"Never miscalculate the abilities of a younger sister," Shelby said with the wisdom of a younger sister.

"Oh," Tanya said. "But my parents don't neglect me; they just have a lot going on with—"

"Of course not," Shelby interrupted her with a smirk. "Case solved." Shelby held out her hand.

Tanya reached into her backpack and pulled out four candy bars and gave them to Shelby.

"Pleasure doing business with you. You may leave now." She dismissed Tanya with a wave of her hand.

Shelby tore open one of the candy bars. "Honestly, Watson, sometimes it takes me longer to explain my findings than to solve a case. Why can't people simply take me at my word? I feel like I've proven myself at this point."

She had, but I liked hearing how she came to her conclusions, especially since there was no way that I would've figured it out. I had a feeling this failure on my part was going to result in more homework from Shelby.

Awesome.

Shelby slumped against her locker. "Is it too much to ask for a nice neighborhood burglary? Or a missing person? My talents are being squandered."

Yep, that's right. Shelby would've preferred our neighborhood be riddled with crooks and kidnappers than have to deal with petty theft. It was clear that Shelby's patience, while barely existing on her best days, was wearing thin.

And okay, I'll admit I was getting a little antsy, too. As

busy as I was, I knew I could always make time for a juicy case.

*Uh-oh.* I was starting to sound just like Shelby.

*That* was not a good sign.

# CHAPTER
# 7

Maybe Shelby was onto something.

The next day in class, Mr. Crosby was acting weird. Really, really weird.

"Okay, so we're going to, ah, look at . . . ," Mr. Crosby said as he began to roll up his sleeves. He stopped suddenly and stared at his left arm for a few moments. He finally blinked and looked at the class as if he didn't realize we were there. "Um, sorry. Where was I?"

"You were discussing the elementary fact that a potato can run a clock," Shelby piped up from the front row. "Although scientists recently discovered that if you boil a potato, it can produce ten times as much energy."

Mr. Crosby stared blankly at her. (Okay, *that* reaction was normal.)

Shelby returned to scribbling in her notebook.

Mr. Crosby pinched the bridge of his nose. "You know, why doesn't everybody turn to chapter six and read to themselves." He collapsed in his chair.

While reading the assignment, I kept looking up at Mr. Crosby. The color had drained from his face, and he was staring at the right side of his desk. Something *was* going on.

I'd never been a huge science fan, but Mr. Crosby had quickly become one of my favorite teachers at the Academy. He'd made it almost fun with experiments like making a battery out of a lemon, using Oreo cookies to study the phases of the moon (no surprise, even Shelby enjoyed that one), and telling time using a water clock.

Once the bell rang, he shook his head like he was trying to get out of his daze.

"What about the work sheet at the end of the chapter?" Shelby asked to the groans of the rest of the class.

"Yes, please have it completed for tomorrow," Mr. Crosby replied with an almost robotic tone.

"Should I turn mine in now?" Shelby held up her finished work sheet; she then placed it on Mr. Crosby's desk before exiting class.

As I walked out of the classroom, I wasn't surprised to see Shelby standing in the hallway.

"See?" she said with a tilt of her head.

"Yeah, okay, but everybody's allowed to have a bad day," I argued.

"But didn't you notice what was missing?"

*Besides* Mr. Crosby's usual energy and class plan?

"His watch!"

"Oh." That was it? People forgot stuff like their watches all the time. Although Mr. Crosby did seem lost without it.

"Don't *oh* me, Watson. Haven't you observed that before we do any experiment in class, Mr. Crosby rolls up his sleeves, removes his watch, and puts it in his locked drawer? It's very important to him."

"Because it tells time?"

"Please be serious, Watson. You of all people should realize the significance of his watch."

Was this a dig because I was three minutes late *one time* to a training session?

"After observing Mr. Crosby's careful behavior regarding his watch, I took note of it. And I realized it was a Bulova A-11 military wristwatch, which was produced in 1943 for the United States government to issue to members of the army and air force. Didn't they teach you any of this on the posts?"

Ah, *no*. Why would anybody know that?

Scratch that. Why would anybody other than Shelby Holmes know that?

Shelby shook her head as she took in my bewildered expression. "*Therefore*, I deduced from Mr. Crosby's age that it was a family heirloom from his great-grandfather who fought in World War II. And now it's missing, and he wasn't acting like someone who simply forgot his watch at home. He's out of sorts. He's confused. He doesn't know what to do. *This* is the piece of the puzzle I've been waiting for." Shelby clapped her hands together. "Don't worry, Watson, I'm going to get to the bottom of this!" She walked down the hallway with a skip in her step.

I wasn't worried, but maybe Mr. Crosby should be.

# CHAPTER
# 8

SHELBY HAD DISAPPEARED AFTER SCHOOL, NO DOUBT ON her quest to blow Mr. Crosby's missing watch out of proportion. Since it was raining, the guys and I headed over to Carlos's after school.

"Who's ready for merciless defeat?" Carlos asked as he held up a controller.

"Oh, so you're peddling fiction like me?" Jason laughed behind his laptop. "I have to finish Watson's latest installment. It's unreal, Watson. And so good."

I'd continued to post my writing journal online every day. Even with insane amounts of homework and Shelby's assignments, I'd found time to obsessively check every ten minutes how many visitors I had to my site. (Hello to my seven readers out there!)

The only problem was, I was running out of Shelby Holmes stories to post. If we didn't get a new case soon, I'd be forced to bring my favorite superhero creation, Sergeant

Speedo, out of retirement. But let's face it, even fictional superheroes couldn't compete with Shelby Holmes (although I would never, and I mean NEVER, tell her that). The few people in class who had read my stuff wanted to hear more about what Shelby could do. I was hoping she'd give me more to write about soon.

"Come on!" Carlos called out. "Or are you a bunch of cowards not wanting to go against me?"

John Wu sat next to Carlos on the floor. " 'Cowards die many times before their deaths; the valiant never taste of death but once.' "

"Yeah, okay, whatever," Carlos replied with a shake of his head. "Actors."

As John and Carlos played, I watched Jason as he read my newest post. It freaked me out to watch someone read my work. But fortunately, Jason was a pretty expressive reader. His eyebrows shot up a lot, and he also laughed, mostly at stuff Shelby had said.

"Chocolate on the cork!" Jason exclaimed with a laugh. "Man, that girl is smart. She makes it look easy."

Yeah, solving crime was pretty easy . . . for Shelby.

"Y'all have got to read Watson's journal," Jason announced, but all eyes were currently glued to the TV where Carlos was giving a play-by-play of John's untimely demise.

"Hey, man, I appreciate you reading it and saying all that

nice stuff," I told Jason. Because it did mean a lot to me. He was really the only person I felt that I could talk to about my writing, except for Ms. Onder, but that was her job. Jason read my stuff because he liked it.

Mom used to read my stories and laugh in all the right spots (and maybe even a few extra places because she's my mom). I hadn't told her about the online journal because then she'd find out what Shelby and I were really up to. At this point, she thought Shelby was simply showing me around or that we were working on schoolwork. Mom told me that I couldn't get involved in Shelby's cases since I shouldn't stick my nose into other people's business. That it would bring nothing but trouble. As far as Mom knew, I hadn't done any sleuthing with Shelby since taking Sir Arthur to the dog show to help with the Lacy case. I hated keeping things from Mom, especially since she'd always been supportive of my writing.

"Of course I'm going to read your stuff, man!" Jason threw his arm around my shoulder. "Us creative types have to stick together. So what's next for the dynamic detective duo of Holmes and Watson?"

"Ah," I mumbled because I had no idea what was going to be next. I didn't know what I was going to post tomorrow. There was no way I could write about Shelby's suspicion about Mr. Crosby since he was a teacher and, you know, there weren't any facts. I was itching for something real to write about (no offense, Sergeant Speedo), so where did that leave me?

There was cheering from Carlos and groaning from John Wu and Bryant in the corner. "Let's go again!" Carlos demanded.

" 'A man can die but once,' " John said as he handed Bryant the controller. "Your turn."

Bryant took the controller and held it up. "No way. I can't tire these fingers out. We got a new Mozart violin sonata in class today." He glared at me. "*Your friend* already had it memorized before class ended."

I simply shrugged in response. Shelby made everybody look bad, especially me.

"Watson!" Carlos called out. "That means you're up next. I know you got army blood and all, but you're about to see what it's like to go against someone who currently has Navy SEAL coursing through his veins." He started up some war game on his TV.

There were many things my mom didn't approve of—junk food, soda, Shelby's cases—but this might be the worst: playing a war-based video game. War, she liked to remind me, was no game. After serving two tours in Afghanistan, and getting injured in combat, she should know.

I reluctantly started to play, even though I had no idea

what I was doing. I couldn't get into it. And it wasn't just disobeying Mom that left me uneasy. Hanging out with the guys was great and all, but I felt restless.

"Dude, are you sleeping or are you playing?" Carlos taunted me as he killed my guy for the second time in as many minutes.

I held it up. "Anybody else want a go?"

Jason saved me as he grabbed the controller, then gave Carlos a taste of his own medicine by not only killing his guy, but upping the trash talk.

John Wu and Bryant laughed, while I remained quiet. I didn't know what was wrong with me. I mean, I was having fun. This was what I wanted: an awesome group of friends. It was a nice, typical afternoon with my dudes.

Still, I was bored. I wanted some adventure, something different.

Maybe it was being in New York City, but I had come to expect something *more* from my downtime.

*Oh no.* It hit me. It wasn't New York City that had changed me. It was being around Shelby.

Shelby Holmes had ruined me for a normal life.

# CHAPTER 9

"How was school?" Mom asked as I entered our first-floor apartment at 221 Baker Street.

"Good. How was work?" I asked as I set my wet backpack down on the floor. It was still pouring outside.

"You're home early." Mom looked at her watch. "I thought you were going to be at Carlos's for a little while longer."

"Yeah, just felt like heading home," I replied with a shrug. Even when the guys decided to switch to a football video game, I didn't have it in me. Virtual reality wasn't cutting it anymore.

"Do you have a lot of homework tonight?" she asked as she opened the fridge.

"Yeah, I'll do it after dinner." I sank down on the couch.

"Are you feeling all right?" Mom put her hand against my forehead. "You didn't drink any soda, did you? Should I check your glucose levels?"

"I'm okay," I told her. "I had some chips and salsa, that's it. I'll do my insulin soon."

"Okay." Mom rubbed her thumb gently on my check. "My baby is growing into such a responsible young man. I'm glad you've settled in so quickly, although you always do."

"Hey, didn't you have a book club at lunch today?" I asked her. "Did you meet any new people?"

I had to keep reminding myself that Mom was starting over, too. She made some friends at work, but she didn't have school to force her to meet new people.

"I did!" She sat down next to me at the kitchen table. "I was all set to talk about the book, but all anybody wanted to discuss was the latest hospital gossip. It was fun, though."

"Did you at least like the book?" I asked.

"Not really, but now I know I don't have to read it for next time."

Mom got up from her chair, walked over to a laundry basket, and pulled out a pair of my jeans. "John, would you care to explain what this is?"

My jeans not only had huge dirt stains on the knees, but there was some plaster stuck on them. I meant to wash them out, but then I was so emotionally scarred from Shelby's "crime scene" that I just balled them up in my closet. I completely forgot about them.

"Oh, yeah." I quickly tried to think of an excuse. "Oh, sorry about that. It was from a science experiment. I got a little sloppy."

She scraped her finger at the plaster. "I don't know if I can get this out. In the future, Mr. Scientist, soak."

I laughed a little louder than I should have. It made me nervous to lie to Mom. I felt bad not telling her everything, but I also wanted to keep working with Shelby. I figured what she didn't know . . .

There was a knock at the door. I quickly went to get it, always intercepting Shelby before she could talk to my mom.

"Hey there, Shelby!"

There was a smirk on her lips. "You're home early," she echoed my mom's exact words. "It appears that an afternoon of staring blindly at a glowing screen with Neanderthals no longer satisfies your intellect like it once did."

But *that* comment was 100 percent grade-A pure Shelby Holmes.

She held up a piece of paper that was crinkled and taped together. "While it never gets old saying that I'm right, you know what is old?"

"Ah." I looked back at Mom, who was listening with interest. "I'm going upstairs to Shelby's. She, um, has a question about homework."

Shelby glared at me. "I certainly do not—"

I walked out into the hallway and shut the door behind us. "Shh," I said to a very annoyed Shelby.

"Watson, there is no way anybody would believe that *I* would need assistance from *you* on our so-called homework."

She had a point. But it was too late to make another excuse.

"I know," I replied in a low whisper as I headed to the stairs. "I just don't want my mom knowing about a case, until, well . . ."

I left it at that. I didn't know when I'd be able to tell Mom about a case, and honestly, Shelby could figure out the details on her own.

Meanwhile, Shelby didn't correct me about having a case. It was about time.

# CHAPTER 10

"HELLO, JOHN!" MR. HOLMES GREETED ME AS WE ENTERED apartment 221B. He was reading a newspaper in one of the armchairs in the living room. "How's school?"

"It's going pretty well, thanks," I replied, much to Shelby's frustration. She was not one for pleasantries (aka normal conversation).

"Is that John?" Mrs. Holmes came down from upstairs. "So lovely to see you! How are you?"

"Ugh!" Shelby stomped her foot. "Must you interrogate Watson every time he comes over? He's clearly faring quite well." Shelby waved her hand up and down me, as if to illustrate how fine I was. "We have important work to do!"

"Shelby!" her father scolded. "We're merely being polite, which is something you need to practice more often."

Shelby had her arms folded. She always seemed so put out by her parents, who were really nice.

"So," her father continued, "if you don't apologize, we're going to have to send you to your room and ask John to leave."

I had to admit it—this was good. Was Shelby really going to swallow her considerable pride and do what her parents wanted?

Shelby exhaled loudly. "Father, Mother, my most sincerest of apologies for reacting so rudely to your inquiries. I must remind myself that you do not possess the same talents and insights as I, so therefore are required to ask redundant questions."

Her parents exchanged a look. For Shelby Holmes, that was about as good of an apology as you could get.

"And don't forget John."

"What about Watson?" Shelby asked.

Yeah, what about me? I didn't do anything wrong!

Her father pushed up his reading glasses. "I believe you owe him an apology as well."

"I certainly do not!" Shelby protested. "Why do I need to apologize to *him*?"

Ah, for starters, maybe for the way she said *to him* with such disregard?

"For your behavior," her dad said through clenched teeth. You didn't need to be a body language expert to see that his patience was wearing thin.

I felt extremely uncomfortable being caught in the

middle. Whatever case Shelby had for us had better be good.

She turned to me, and I could tell that she was not happy about having to apologize.

Hmm. Suddenly I began to enjoy this. Shelby didn't like to say sorry for anything, so I planned to stockpile this one for when she really *did* need to apologize (and her parents wouldn't be there to force her).

"Watson, I'm so, so, *so* sorry for my horrific behavior. Will you ever be able to forgive me?" Her voice was laced with so much fake sugar, my teeth hurt.

"I believe I can find it in my heart to forgive you," I replied with a smile on my face that infuriated her even further.

"Now that I've properly paid penance for my misdeeds, I need to discuss a rather urgent matter with Watson. We'll be in the kitchen." Shelby led me past the dining room to their kitchen, which matched ours one floor below. "First, I really do need to apologize to you, Watson. For real this time."

This was a record: two apologies in one evening!

"I'm sorry you had to witness that altercation with my parents. They do mean well, but their attempts at training me to be a mindless nitwit are in vain."

So she had set a new record in apologies—that ended up insulting someone. It was her specialty.

Shelby held up the crinkled and taped piece of paper she'd shown me downstairs. "Tell me, who wrote this?"

Aw man. This wasn't about a case. This was only one of her tests.

But wait. The paper was covered in something. And it smelled. It looked like something she dug out of the trash.

"Yeah, I'm not touching that thing," I said as I pulled my hand away.

"Stop being such a prude," Shelby reprimanded me as she forced the piece of paper on me.

On the paper were only a few lines of text.

**I don't understand why you would do this to me. Can we please talk this out and find some sort of compromise? I can't do what you're asking. I'm begging for at least an explanation of why this is happening.**

"So, who wrote it?" she asked.

The dark brown stain on the letter could've been from a drink. Coffee, maybe?

"An adult?" I guessed.

"Yes, very good, Watson!" Shelby pointed to the letter again. "But don't you see it?"

"The coffee stain?" I mean, there wasn't much to see besides the big stain and that the letter had been ripped into several pieces. "The person tore it up because they didn't want anybody to see it."

"Yes," Shelby replied. "I should be grateful he doesn't have a shredder."

*It's a* he? Hold on. Did this mean that this wasn't a Shelby test, but an actual clue to a real case? And why did I have a sinking feeling in my stomach that this had to do with Mr. Crosby.

"But wait, there's more!" Shelby reached into her back pocket and produced a piece of lined notebook paper.

"During my preliminary investigation of a possible crime scene, I noticed that a piece of paper was ripped out of a notebook. So I used a rather pedestrian method to discover what had been written."

She handed me the paper. There, peeking up between shading Shelby had done with a pencil, was Detective Lestrade's name and phone number. "Detective Lestrade?"

"Yes! Oh, how I'd love to show her up. Yet again."

Shelby's current giddy demeanor made sense. Lestrade was Shelby's enemy. Their relationship pretty much went like this: Shelby usually knew more about a case than the actual New York City detective, and Lestrade would dismiss Shelby.

Yet, I still had no idea what the one letter and the detective's phone number had to do with each other. Or with Mr. Crosby.

"Okay, okay," I said as I tried to put the pieces together. "The person who wrote this letter needs Detective Lestrade for something?"

"Yes, but why call the so-called 'police' when there isn't a crime that we can't solve?"

As much as I wanted to work on a case, I didn't want to get involved in anything serious enough for the police.

"Once again, Watson, who wrote this letter? Because he is our next client."

There was no way it could be Crosby, could it? She'd been poking around his office. But it didn't make sense. The letter didn't mention anything about a watch.

I took a closer look at the letter. It was on a standard piece of paper. The person used the basic Times New Roman font. There weren't any other clues.

"What have I been telling you? You need to not just see, but observe."

"I have been observing," I defended myself. There wasn't much to *observe*—the letter was basic black and white. Literally. Well, except for the brown stain.

"Really?" Shelby leaned against the kitchen counter. "How many times have you come up the stairs to see me?"

"Was I supposed to count?"

"No, but would you say that you have come up a few times a week since you've been here?"

"Yes." Where was she going with this?

"Okay, so how many steps are there?"

"What?" I blurted out.

"You've climbed those stairs at least several dozen times, yet you never noticed how many steps there are?"

I was stunned. She was right. (OF COURSE SHE WAS!) I've gone up and down those stairs tons of times, but never paid close attention to them. "I guess . . ."

"You should never guess, especially if facts are present."

"Do you want me to go and count?"

She sighed heavily. "No, I want you to observe."

"Twelve!" I threw out a random number because I wanted to get back to discussing the case.

"While that is a good *guess* since twelve is the average number of steps for a staircase, there are fourteen steps. I won't even bother asking you about the design of the carpet, but do try a little harder when it comes to observing, Watson."

"Okay." Now I was trying to remember what the carpet looked like. It had some kind of design, like, um, flowers? I had no idea. It had blue in it. Maybe gray? Wow. I really hadn't been paying too much attention to where I lived. What hope did I have in solving cases if I hadn't even noticed the carpet I walked on every day?

Shelby held the paper up to the light. "First, this paper is very flimsy. Not high-quality stock. It's the kind that's bought in large quantities at an office or school. However, the big thing you're missing is that there's something very familiar with the inconsistency of the ink printer. See the lighter printing on the right side?"

Shelby traced a line down the paper, and I saw she was right. There was a slight difference between the darkness of the letters on either side of it.

"You don't recognize the printing deficiency?"

I shook my head.

"Oh, Watson, you really need to study your homework closer."

*Homework*? She hadn't given me any assignments about printing and ink yet. What homework was she talking about?

"Well," Shelby said as she threw her hands up like she was giving up on me (at this point, I wouldn't blame her, I'd missed so much already), "we need to leave for school thirty minutes early tomorrow."

"Why?"

"To talk to our new client. Someone clearly needs our help, and better us than Lestrade."

Shelby laughed at my confused expression. "What did I say when I knocked on your door? It doesn't get old being right. But what does get old is when people doubt me. Even you."

She handed me another piece of paper, this one with our science homework on it. Before I could ask her why she was showing me this, I saw it. It was so slight that it made perfect sense that I missed it before. The homework had the same printing inconsistency as the letter.

"Yes, Watson, it appears that Mr. Crosby has something to hide, indeed."

# CHAPTER 11

THIS WAS A BAD IDEA.

Even if the letter was something Crosby had written or received, and Shelby was convinced it was, that didn't mean he needed our help. Or even wanted it. He was a teacher. We were his students. There were certain lines that shouldn't be crossed.

But none of that was going to stop Shelby.

As much as I was itching for a case and something new to write about, there was no way this was going to end well.

"We shouldn't be doing this," I said for the fortieth time that morning as we walked into school. "Maybe we should write him a letter or something."

Shelby paused before entering Crosby's classroom. Whoa, was Shelby actually going to listen to me?

"Feel free to stay out here," she said before opening the door and walking in.

No. Of course she wasn't.

I sighed and followed her. Like I was going to miss whatever was about to happen.

Mr. Crosby looked up from his desk, and I swear there was a flash of panic on his face. He quickly put a friendly smile in its place. "Well, good morning, Shelby and John. What can I do for you?"

Shelby strode over to his desk. "I understand some adults may consider it awkward to ask a preadolescent for help, but I'm here to assist you with your little problem."

Mr. Crosby's eyes darted to me, then he cleared his throat. "I'm afraid I don't know what you're talking about. Is this about yesterday's assignment?"

Shelby sat down in her usual seat at the front of the classroom, while I sat next to her. "Let me explain to you what I do, Mr. Crosby. I help people. Granted, they usually come to *me* so this is a rather unorthodox start, but you clearly seem to be in a situation that requires my assistance. Am I right?"

Mr. Crosby glanced again at me.

"You can trust Watson, Mr. Crosby. He's been surprisingly adequate in helping me on occasion."

*Gee, thanks, Shelby.*

Mr. Crosby hadn't moved a muscle since we walked in.

"I think there's been some mistake," Crosby said, but there was panic in his eyes.

"I see that your watch is still missing, which is a shame,"

Shelby said as she folded her hands on the desk. "Not only because it's a precious family heirloom, but it is worth a considerable amount. Around five hundred dollars last time I checked."

One time, years ago, Dad and I were driving home to the base in Kentucky through woods when he slammed on the brakes. There was a deer in the middle of the road that was frozen with fear, eyes wide. Mr. Crosby had the exact same expression on his face now.

"Finding a stolen watch is a rather easy task, Mr. Crosby." Shelby glanced at the clock. "You've got two minutes before I walk out of this room, and my skills will be accompanying me."

After a few seconds of awkward silence, Crosby finally broke. "It's not that simple."

"Even better," Shelby said as a smile spread on her lips. "I like my cases with a few twists and turns."

While the thought of a complicated case gave me a headache.

"Listen, the last thing I wanted to do was get you involved, but you should probably know what's going on since it concerns you."

*WHAT?* How did Mr. Crosby's missing watch have anything to do with Shelby?

However, if this news surprised Shelby, she didn't show

it. She leaned back in her chair and closed her eyes. "Tell me everything."

"I guess I should start at the beginning," Crosby said as he unlocked a drawer in his desk. He handed us a few pieces of paper.

The first one was an e-mail sent to him a week before school started.

Dear Mason,

Congratulations on your new position at the Harlem Academy of the Arts. I must inform you that if you don't fail one of your students, Shelby Holmes, I will be forced to contact the administrators and tell them what a horrible teacher you were and get your position revoked. Do it as soon as possible before it's too late for you.

Ms. Semple

Who was this Ms. Semple, and what did she want with Shelby? Why would she want Shelby to fail a class? It didn't make sense. And it didn't mention a watch.

"This is out of character for Ms. Semple," Shelby replied with furrowed brows as she examined the letter closer.

"How do you know this Ms. Semple person?" I asked.

"She's the headmistress at Miss Adler's School, where Mr. Crosby taught before coming here."

"Okay, but how do you know her? Or I guess I should ask, how does she know *you*?"

Shelby shrugged. "I went to Miss Adler's for first grade and stayed two years before transferring here."

"You did?" I'd assumed Shelby had always gone to the Academy.

"I must've just missed you there," Mr. Crosby replied.

"I'm surprised you hadn't heard of me when you arrived," Shelby boasted. "I found the school to be a little too uptight for me. But oh how Ms. Semple had begged me to stay. They kept throwing scholarship money at me and bumped me up yet another grade, but there wasn't anything they could do to keep me."

"Wait a second," Mr. Crosby said with a laugh. "I do remember when I got there they talked about this girl who aced her entrance exam. That was you?"

"Did they happen to mention that I found a *mistake* on their 'exam' as well?" Shelby used air quotes when she said the word *exam*, her opinion of the difficulty of the exam pretty clear. "Amateurs. They're lucky they even got me to attend in the first place, let alone grace them with my presence for two years. But it looks like Ms. Semple wants me back. How desperate for her to resort to blackmail."

Mr. Crosby cleared his throat. "Well, I took care of it. I

went straight to Principal Loh when I received this letter. I told Ms. Semple that I would not bow down to her threats."

"You spoke with her?" Shelby asked.

"No, I replied to her e-mail. I wanted all of this to be in writing. Listen, I've always been an upstanding person, and feel like I've proven myself to be a good teacher."

"You have!" I piped in.

"You've been competent," Shelby replied with a sniff.

(I mean, honestly, that's a compliment coming from her.)

"So that's it?" I asked, wondering why he would tell us this if it had been taken care of.

"No," Shelby replied. "That's not it. After Mr. Crosby informed Ms. Semple he wouldn't fall for petty blackmail, she stole his watch. Do I even need to ask if I'm right?"

Crosby slumped in his seat. "I returned from lunch yesterday to this letter on my desk." He handed us another letter.

**Mason, I don't think you realize how serious I am. Fail Shelby Holmes or you'll never see your watch again.**

"I went in my drawer and it was gone."

"This was why you were going to contact Detective Lestrade," Shelby stated to Mr. Crosby's surprise.

"Yes, I was going to talk to her today. This has gotten out of hand. It's not simply the watch, which is very important to my family. I'm not going to give in to blackmail." Crosby grimaced. "This has all been so confusing. I don't understand why Ms. Semple would go through all of this just so I would fail you. Do you really think this is all so you'd go back there?"

"Well, it was a coup for Miss Adler's when I decided to attend. Every school wanted me after my test scores. I'm not surprised she'd go to such lengths to get me to return. As if a school could fail me in anything."

That was true, since schools didn't grade on things like *humility*.

While Shelby seemed pretty pleased with herself, it didn't add up to me. "But why would she blackmail Mr. Crosby instead of coming to you directly? Even if you failed science, and then, for some reason, had to leave the Academy, it wouldn't necessarily mean you'd go back there."

"Never underestimate a headmistress scorned."

Shelby's ego, which was always higher than average, was above and beyond now. "I don't know, Shelby. It seems like a bit much," I said.

Shelby glared at me, more so than normal, which I assumed meant that I'd offended her. Although it was kind of nice to give her a taste of her own medicine. But I knew my questions poked holes in her theory: Why would the head of a school resort to blackmail? And wouldn't she blackmail Shelby? Why involve Mr. Crosby?

"I realize this must be very hard on you, Mr. Crosby." Shelby sat up straighter in her seat. "But let me assure you that I've got this."

"No, no," Mr. Crosby said as he stood up. "I will not have you get involved. I'll talk to Detective Lestrade, and it will be taken care of."

Shelby began to laugh. "You think Detective Lestrade will get to the bottom of this? It would be my absolute pleasure to retrieve your watch."

"I can't have you—"

"Give me until Monday afternoon."

"What do you mean? Do you know where the watch is?"

"This should be fairly easy." Shelby got up from her chair and began pacing the room. "When one has an item of value, especially one involved in blackmail, they want to keep it near them. Ms. Semple most likely has it with her at school. While I am currently unaware of the location of her safe, she certainly has one in her office. That would be the most logical place she'd keep the watch. She wears a key to something around her neck; it must be to a safe."

"How do you know that?" Mr. Crosby asked.

"Because I pay attention. Although Ms. Semple is a lot

more cautious than you have been. It's not surprising that someone knew how to get to your watch. You practically wave around your key ring with the red plastic key cover to denote which one opens your desk drawer."

"But I had my keys on me," Mr. Crosby argued.

"*Pfft!*" Shelby rolled her eyes. "Your desk drawer lock is a joke."

Mr. Crosby looked at Shelby with great concern. "So you're saying that Ms. Semple came in here yesterday and picked my lock while I was at lunch."

Shelby shook her head. "She couldn't risk getting spotted. She probably had some help. Oh! Maybe it's even someone on the inside." Shelby continued to walk around the room with even more manic energy. "Yes, this was exactly what I needed. Please, Mr. Crosby, you have to give me a couple days to come up with a plan and retrieve your watch. Let me at least do that. I want nothing more than to best Ms. Semple's plan. Then *after* I've been successful, you can talk to Lestrade about Semple's letters."

I couldn't help but think that Shelby also wanted to best Detective Lestrade. And, okay, I was looking forward to having a case (and something to write about), even though I was still uneasy about a few things. Mostly that this wasn't as simple as Shelby made it seem. I had so many questions, but Shelby's enthusiasm for the case was starting to spread.

"I don't know . . ." Mr. Crosby looked pained.

"Come on! I've been itching for a good undercover case." Shelby was bouncing back and forth on her heels.

"Undercover?"

"Yes! As you know, we have Monday off next week for teacher in-service. Since Miss Adler's is a private school, class will be in session. I'll pay her a visit then and retrieve your watch. I'll have it in your hands in no time!"

"No, no." Mr. Crosby shook his head. "I can't ask you to do that."

"You're not. I'm volunteering my services. After all, shouldn't I be involved since this has to do with me? You wouldn't be in this mess if I weren't such an amazing student."

All Mr. Crosby could do was nod in agreement.

She stood in front of him. "I insist on helping you, Mr. Crosby. Let me make this right. I'll return your watch by Monday afternoon. After that, I'll even go with you to discuss the blackmail situation with Detective Lestrade. Then you and I can both put Miss Adler's behind us. Deal?"

Shelby extended her hand across Mr. Crosby's desk. It took a moment for Crosby to finally shake it. "Deal. As long as you know what you're doing."

Shelby raised her eyebrow at him for even questioning that.

"And please be careful. I realize you have special skills and that you want to be involved, but you are just a student."

"But I'm not *just* a student," Shelby said with a smirk. "Ask Ms. Semple."

"You really want to do this?" he asked with a shake of his head.

"Of course! What's better than going undercover at the very school that's desperate to have me and getting your watch back?"

Mr. Crosby started laughing. "Okay, okay. But be careful. *Both* of you."

I gave him a smile since I was still confused about several things, except that on Monday we'd be extracting a watch. All right, I was getting excited. I'd never gone undercover before. My mind was buzzing with all the different ways I could write about our adventure.

"Now, Mr. Crosby, while I am volunteering my *services*, going undercover does incur some expenses." She batted her eyelashes at him.

"Oh, of course." Crosby took out his wallet.

This was new. I'd never seen Shelby take cash before. She preferred to be paid in chocolate. But I guessed if she was going to go undercover at some fancy girls' school, she was going to need some expensive items.

"Twenty should do, for now." She held out her hand while

Mr. Crosby gave her the bills. "Mark my word, Mr. Crosby, your watch will be returned in no time."

"Thank you, I really appreciate it."

"Just one more thing, Mr. Crosby," Shelby said as she was heading out the door. "You may want to fix the toner in your printer."

# CHAPTER
## 12

I COULDN'T WAIT FOR SCHOOL TO BE OVER SO WE COULD come up with a plan for Monday. Well, that was what I was hoping. But as Shelby and I made our way home, she was completely silent. Every once in a while, she'd mutter something under her breath. I wanted to pepper her with questions, but figured she needed some time to put everything together.

Once we got to our block, she kept walking. "Ah, Shelby?" I called after her, but she didn't turn around. I jogged to catch up with her. "Where are you going?"

"Need to talk to . . . ," she mumbled. At least I *think* that was what she said. So I deduced we were on our way to talk with one of Shelby's contacts.

Most of her contacts were people in our neighborhood, although one time we met with a bookie in a really scary part of town. To my relief, she bypassed the 125th Street subway and kept walking downtown.

After a couple more blocks, I couldn't take the silence anymore. "Is it really going to be that easy to retrieve Mr. Crosby's watch?"

Shelby snorted, and we crossed 120th Street. "Yes. Ms. Semple won't be expecting some sweet lil' ol' fourth grader on a school tour to take her down. This is going to be fun, Watson."

Again, Shelby and I have very different definitions of the word *fun*. Although I was looking forward to this. It *could* be fun.

"But won't you need a parent to go with you?" When I got a tour of the Academy, Mom was with me. She did everything regarding school, actually. All I had to do was show up.

"While *some* kids may require a parent to chaperone them to a school interview, I'm going by myself. I'll write a letter as my alter ego's mother saying that I'm a fiercely independent young girl, whose decision to attend is mine alone, therefore I'll be doing the interview on my own."

"Is that really going to work?"

"It did when I originally went there."

I stopped dead in my tracks. "Wait a second. You did your interviews *for first grade* by yourself?"

Shelby kept walking. "Of course I did. Did you think I was really going to have *my parents* decide where I was going to attend school?"

Yes. Yes, I did. Because that's what every single other child from the beginning of time has done when it came to first grade. Not like I had a choice of where I was going to go to school at that age, since there was only one elementary school on the post. But still . . .

"What's Ms. Semple like?" I asked. I kept picturing a villain from some movie: evil laugh, smoking a cigarette from some long holder, petting a hairless cat on her lap. She had to be horrible to do something like this, right?

Shelby scrunched her face as if she was putting something complicated together. "Single woman in her midfifties, has been in the academic world all her life: first as a student, then a teacher, and now as headmistress. Never married, but always considered her students to be her own children. I will admit that I do find this behavior rather against her character. However, as I've learned so many times prior to this case, appearances can be deceiving."

"How are you going to find out where the safe is?" I asked.

"Oh, that part will be easy. The better question, Watson, is how am I going to get Ms. Semple out of her office so I can steal the watch?"

"Do you know how you're going to get that key from her necklace?"

"I don't need the key. I'm going to pick the lock."

"You really know how to *pick locks*?" I'd assumed she was simply bragging when she made that comment about Mr. Crosby's desk lock. (I should've known better by now.)

"How else do you expect me to retrieve something from a locked compartment? Ah, finally," Shelby said as she looked up at a small storefront with a blissful expression.

"Levain Bakery," I read the blue sign aloud. "You have a contact here?"

"Contact?" Shelby said as she opened the door. "No, I need some inspiration."

We walked in and the smell of freshly baked cookies made my mouth water. There wasn't a lot of room in front of the glass bakery case that took up most of the width of the store, but behind it there were six different bakers scooping out huge dollops of cookie dough onto baking sheets.

Since I grew up not really being able to eat a lot of sweets, I've never craved them like Shelby. Well, I doubted *anybody* ate sweets like Shelby. But I had to admit seeing those huge gooey cookies made me jealous.

Shelby stood in line. "Do you want anything?" she asked.

My response was a glare. I mean, really? I wanted everything, but Mom wouldn't have approved. I could only get away with so much. Yeah, she'd believe a white lie about plaster on my pants, but there was no way I could fudge my glucose levels.

Shelby began pointing to all the items she was ordering. I couldn't help but laugh because this was the happiest I'd ever seen her. Her nose was practically pressed up against the case as she studied each item with a huge grin on her face. I had to remember that all it took to put her in a good mood was to be surrounded by sugar.

"So what's the plan?" I asked as her items were being bagged.

She pulled a large chocolate peanut butter chip cookie out of the bag and took a huge bite. "It's starting to come together."

Shelby handed the cashier Mr. Crosby's money.

"Wait. *That's* what the money's for?" I asked. "Shouldn't we be using it for disguises or something?"

"Never doubt the power of sugar!" Shelby declared as we exited the bakery and headed back uptown.

Did she really need to say that to a diabetic?

"There are many things we have to consider, Watson," Shelby said before shoving the remainder of the ginormous cookie into her mouth. Shelby chewed vigorously, then gave me a smile. "I hope you don't mind spending your day off working. I'm going to need your help."

"Of course!" I replied with a laugh. I think this was the

first time Shelby had ever *asked* me for help. I was always ready to get involved.

"Great!" Shelby said as she licked chocolate off her hand. "Because you are going to play a vital role in this case, Watson. Without you I'm afraid I'd be pretty useless inside the school. I need someone on the outside to do a very crucial task."

"Awesome!"

"I have it all figured out, but being able to successfully retrieve Mr. Crosby's watch from Ms. Semple's safe will require everything to go precisely as planned. There are many ways things could go wrong. But I'm not worried. I know you're the right man for the job, Watson."

"I sure am! I'm up for anything!" I was feeling pretty confident as we waited for the walk signal at 125th Street. When I first started working with Shelby, she questioned my talents. But no longer! I was her man! We had this!

"Splendid, Watson! I knew that I could count on you. We're not going to let something trivial like the law get in the way of this case."

*Wait. WHAT?!*

Shelby continued, oblivious to the look of panic that had appeared suddenly on my face. "So happy you aren't worried about a tiny thing like getting arrested. All part of the job!"

The walk sign lit up and Shelby bounced across the street, while I stood there frozen as people maneuvered around me.

What exactly had I gotten myself into?

# ᘒ CHAPTER ᘒ
# 13

"YO, WATSON!" JASON CALLED OUT TO ME. "ARE YOU playing ball or what?"

"Sorry," I replied as I shook my head to get all my worries out of my mind. It was Saturday morning, and I was playing baseball at Marcus Garvey Park with Jason and Carlos. John Wu was rehearsing for a play, and Bryant was convinced if he practiced more, he could finally one-up Shelby in music class. While I applauded the guy's commitment to violin, I didn't have the heart to tell him it was pretty impossible to beat Shelby in anything.

I had thought that spending a few hours tossing around a ball would clear my head. It ended up giving me more time to think, and worry, about Monday.

Even though there wasn't a lot for me to think about since I still had no idea what I was going to be doing. And I mean *no idea*. Every time I asked Shelby, she'd simply reply that she was working on it and it would be really simple and "*technically* not illegal." Oh, yeah, she also said that my "safety wasn't going to be in jeopardy."

Somehow that didn't comfort me.

"Watson?" Jason waved his arms around to get my attention.

So much for taking my mind off things.

"How about a break?" I called out.

"Yeah," Jason replied. He jogged over to me with Carlos behind him. "We got to figure out what we're going to do on Monday."

"Oh, I know," Carlos said. He lifted his chin at me. "We need to take Army Dude to hallowed ground."

"What do you think, Watson?" Jason asked. "You must be dying to go to Rucker's."

"What's Rucker's?" I asked.

"No way, man!" Carlos threw his hands up. "Please do not tell me you've never heard of Rucker Park?"

"Ah, clearly," I said as I punched him on the shoulder. "So you got me. What am I missing?"

"Okay, okay." Carlos wrapped his arm around my neck. "Let me educate you. The legends, the greats—Dr. J and Chamberlain, Kobe and LeBron—have all played there. Kevin Durant lit up the place with sixty-six points during *one game*. This is where the elite practice their skills. It's *the* place to play basketball in New York City. Let all those Wall

Street poseurs have the West 4th Street court. We'll take Rucker's. The best part: it's in Harlem."

"Whoa," I said in awe. I knew there were a ton of historic places in New York City and my neighborhood. I've walked by the Apollo Theater a few times, and Mom told me that a lot of big acts got their start there, like Michael Jackson when he was with his brothers in the Jackson 5. But I thought the only big-time places to play ball were at stadiums like Madison Square Garden. It was amazing that such an important court was in Harlem. And that I could actually play there.

"Usually it's hard to get into a pickup game on the weekend," Carlos continued. "The dudes that hang there are always older, taller, faster, and better. But on Monday morning it should be pretty dead. We can finally have our time."

Jason and Carlos high-fived each other. I joined in until I realized I had something else to do on Monday. What that was, I had no idea, but as much fun as a good game of basketball could be (especially on sacred ground), nothing could match the rush of being on a case with Shelby.

"Ah, this Monday?" I asked, even though I knew the answer.

"Um, yeah, *this Monday*," Carlos said as he nudged me. "What other Monday do we have off?"

"I can't." I hung my head in disappointment.

Unless maybe I could do both? I knew Shelby and I were going to the school in the morning, but the way she made it sound, we weren't going to be there all day.

"What about the afternoon?" I suggested, not wanting to miss out.

"No way. It'll be too busy then. Morning's the best shot. What do you got going on Monday?"

Mom had asked me that same question last night. I'd told her that Shelby was going to take me to the Museum of Natural History. Even though I'd been in New York for almost two months, Mom still didn't trust me to wander too far away from the apartment or school by myself. Since Shelby had been living here her entire life, Mom didn't mind if I went places with her. As long as I wasn't working on one of her cases.

I was going to be in so much trouble if she ever found out the truth.

"I have a doctor's appointment," I lied. If I told them I was working with Shelby, the guys would pump me for details. While I wanted them to know I was doing some cool sleuthing or whatever, I had to keep it a secret since Mr. Crosby was involved. Maybe I could meet up afterward and tell them about how we saved the day.

"That's a shame, man." Jason swung his bat to warm up. "Just text me when you're done, oh . . ."

Yeah, I couldn't text him because Mom still refused to let

me have a cell phone. Everybody else in my grade seemed to have one.

"I'll give you a call when I'm done," I said, trying to not shudder from embarrassment.

"Sure, sure." Jason took a practice swing. "Let's get back to it."

Carlos threw me the ball, and I went to the pitcher's mound. I took the baseball in my hand, wound up for the pitch, and let the ball fly. Jason swung, and the ball went sailing past Carlos's head in the outfield.

"Nice job, man!" I called to Jason as he took a victorious lap around the bases, pumping his fists in the air.

I relaxed as I decided to focus on the positive: I was having fun with my new friends. They were great. School was going well.

Now all I needed was for things to go smoothly on Monday. That whatever I was going to do wouldn't land me in jail.

Or worse, grounded.

# CHAPTER 14

"THERE YOU ARE, JOHN!" MRS. HUDSON CALLED OUT TO ME as I started climbing the steps to the front door of our building. "I have someone I want you to meet!"

I really wanted to shower after playing in the park, but I turned around and headed down the stairs to her garden apartment. I'd only been in Mrs. Hudson's place a couple of times. I really didn't know a lot about her except that she was originally from Colombia, and that there didn't seem to be a Mr. Hudson. Her apartment had the exact same layout as our apartment above, except that she had access to the garden in the backyard.

"John," Mrs. Hudson said as I entered the living room, "this is my niece, Becky."

A white girl with straight black bangs and chin-length hair, who was around seven or eight years old, sat as stiff as a board on the sofa with her legs crossed at her ankles. She had on a plaid dress and white cardigan, paired with white knee-high socks and black patent leather shoes. I looked back and forth between her and Mrs. Hudson trying to see the resemblance. They shared the same tanned-skin complexion, but that was about it. Mrs. Hudson always had her hair pulled into a messy bun and wore flowing dresses and skirts. This girl seemed way too uptight to be related.

"Hello, John," Becky said with a quiet, high-pitched voice. "It's lovely to meet you. Auntie has said so many wonderful things about you and your mother."

"Thanks," I replied. I felt uncomfortable just standing there, so I sat on the chair opposite her, wondering how long I'd have to stay.

"Why don't I get you some milk and cookies," Mrs. Hudson said before she disappeared into the kitchen.

"So where are you from?" I asked. "Do you live around here?"

"Oh heavens no, I wish! I live in boring old New Jersey, but I love visiting my auntie. How long have you lived here?"

"Almost two months."

"So you must've met the Holmeses, then." She gave me a shy smile.

"Yeah, they're really great."

Mrs. Hudson walked in and placed a plate of cookies and two glasses of milk on the coffee table before retreating to the kitchen. Becky carefully picked up a cookie and took the smallest bite out of hers, chewing it slowly. My stomach growled from my morning with the guys. I decided Mom would be okay with me having a cookie since these were about a tenth the size of those at Levain Bakery. I took a big bite, hoping that with a full mouth I wouldn't be expected to say anything. I usually didn't have a problem making small talk (moving from army post to army post made you quick at making friends), but I wasn't used to being around someone so prim and proper. I felt like I was having tea with royalty.

"Auntie mentioned that you work with Shelby on some cases."

I finished chewing before replying, "Yeah, we're partners."

"That must be interesting." Becky took another tiny nibble of her cookie. Apparently the guys at school weren't the only ones who wanted to know what it was like to work with Shelby. If only more people were reading my online journal. I barely had twenty readers.

"Yes, it's never a dull moment with Shelby, that's for

sure." I debated how much to tell her. I didn't want Becky visiting my mom and spilling my secrets.

Becky gave a very girly giggle and covered her mouth. "I'm sure that's true. Auntie sometimes refers to her as A Big Handful in a Tiny Package."

I laughed loudly. "You have no idea."

Becky grimaced, in a very familiar and disturbing way. Then I watched as she slumped back, kicked off her shoes, and rammed the rest of the cookie into her mouth. "Et tu, Watson?"

*Wait a second.* I stood up and examined Becky from head to feet. She still looked the same, but her entire demeanor had changed.

"It's safe to enter now, Mrs. Hudson!" Becky called out, but in a different voice. A very familiar voice. A sickening feeling started to take over my stomach, one that had nothing to do with the cookie I inhaled.

Mrs. Hudson came out of the kitchen clapping her hands. "This is all so exciting, I could hardly keep a straight face! I don't know how you do it, Shelby!"

*SHELBY?!*

"Well, it's clear my disguise works. Although I don't know why on earth you felt the need to change my name." Shelby reached up and pulled a wig off her head.

"I'm sorry, Shelby, but I couldn't remember that silly name you came up with."

"There's nothing silly about Basia Rathbone," Shelby remarked. "An unusual name is an easy one for a mark to forget or misremember."

Mrs. Hudson looked impressed. "Oh, you think of everything, Shelby! I'm glad I could help, especially since you're being so brave helping your teacher." Mrs. Hudson turned to me, but I was still in shock over Shelby's transformation. "What do you think of my handiwork, John? I was thrilled when Shelby asked me for a makeover."

"It's not a makeover, it's a disguise," Shelby protested.

"Of course, dear." Mrs. Hudson patted Shelby on the head, but Shelby swatted her hand away. "Let me get you some more milk!" She headed toward the kitchen, leaving me alone again with "Basia."

I knelt down in front of Shelby to study her face. "So it's makeup?" I asked. Gone were Shelby's freckles and porcelain skin.

"It's makeup and a wig, but most of all it's a commitment to a character. I don't just dress up, I *become*: voice, posture, body language, everything." Shelby took a giant bite of a cookie.

Honestly, out of everything I witnessed, the fact that Shelby was able to take tiny nibbles as "Becky" or "Basia" or whoever was probably the most impressive. *That* was commitment!

"On Monday morning, Basia Rathbone has an interview

with Ms. Semple about possibly attending Miss Adler's. She fell for the e-mail I sent as Basia's mother. Everything's in place and working according to my detailed plan."

"Cool! Do I need an alias for Monday?" I started to get excited about who I could pretend to be. I really needed to start paying attention to how other people carried themselves so I could fully *become* someone else like Shelby had.

"Not this time."

"Oh." I didn't bother to hide my disappointment.

I looked over to the kitchen door, unsure how much Mrs. Hudson knew. "Does Mrs. Hudson know everything?"

I was nervous about Mrs. Hudson bumping into my mom in the hallway and discussing our cases, specifically my involvement in them. Plus, there was a little pang of jealousy that Shelby trusted someone else to help with her cases.

"Mrs. Hudson is strictly on a need-to-know basis," Shelby replied as she scratched her head, making her usual unruly hair stick up even more. "She used to buy me flowery hair bands, so she was thrilled that I asked her to make me look like a Miss Adler's girl." Shelby looked down at her outfit with disgust.

"Didn't you have to dress up when you went there?"

"Yes." Shelby pretended to gag. "I was required to wear their uniform, but I wasn't happy about it. And I didn't bother with things like perfect hair or being a girly girl.

Miss Adler's couldn't brainwash me into turning into their version of the perfect student: quiet, well behaved, and, worst of all, boring. But that is all in the past. On Monday I'm not Shelby Holmes; I have to be Basia Rathbone. Ms. Semple can't know it's me."

"Well, it worked with me," I replied. Shelby really didn't look anything like herself. "Hey, so do you know how long it's going to take at the school? I was hoping that I could join the guys to play some ball after we're done."

"Shouldn't be a problem. We won't be more than an hour at Miss Adler's. It'll be quick and easy."

My mood instantly improved. I was going to be able to do both things: solve crime and play basketball! Everything was going to be okay.

Shelby shrugged her shoulders. "It's truly remarkable how panicky people can get in a fire."

WAIT.

WHAT?

WHO SAID ANYTHING ABOUT A FIRE?

# ⁓ CHAPTER ⁓
# 15

No, I wasn't going to start a fire.

At least, as Shelby kept assuring me, I wasn't *technically* starting a fire.

Guess how much that comforted me?

Yep. Zilch.

"It's simply a device that lets out a lot of smoke, not fire," Shelby explained as she stood on a step stool in her kitchen on Sunday afternoon. She was stirring some weird mixture on the stove. It looked like peanut butter. "It's the *appearance* of fire. This is a very simple science experiment."

*Simple for who exactly?*

"Figured it must be you in the kitchen with that odor." Shelby's older brother, Michael, entered with Shelby's English bulldog, Sir Arthur, trailing after him. "Do I even want to speculate as to what you're doing?"

"You could, but I doubt you'd come close," Shelby replied with a glare.

You could say that Shelby and her brother have your typical sibling rivalry, although there's nothing typical about either of them. Michael's only sixteen, but recently started his freshman year at Columbia University.

Michael turned to me. "My baby sister is always under the impression that her intelligence is greater than it actually is. Yet here she is making an elementary concoction, while I'm learning a great deal at the *university.*"

I tried not to laugh since Shelby was mimicking Michael behind his back.

"For instance," Michael continued unaware, "we spent all last week studying natural energy. Did *you* know that a bolt of lightning is five times hotter than the surface of the sun?"

Ah, *no. Why* would I know that?

"Did your *college professor* forget to mention that the surface of the sun is its coolest layer," Shelby added dryly. "At the core, plasma temperatures can reach about fifteen million kelvins."

Michael narrowed his eyes at her. "Oh, really?"

I sat on the floor rubbing Sir Arthur's belly, knowing that they could spew random science factoids at each other for a while.

"I'm simply stating facts."

"How unenlightening," Michael replied in his usual monotone voice, but there was an edge of irritation.

"Let's see," Shelby said as she tapped her chin with her finger. "What else can I educate you on, dear brother. A full head of human hair is strong enough to support twelve metric tons."

"Well, did you know that it would take you precisely forty-two minutes and twelve seconds to travel through the earth if someone drilled a hole from one end to the other?"

I raised my hand because I felt like I was in class. "Okay, but *how* do people know that? Like, nobody actually drilled a hole into the earth and jumped through."

Both Shelby and Michael looked at me like *I* had just said something completely crazy.

"It's a proven scientific fact," Michael replied with a scowl that closely resembled Shelby's.

"So by proven, you mean someone really did jump through the earth?"

Michael tilted his head like he was trying to decipher if I was making a joke. I wasn't. I really wanted to understand exactly how they knew that. I'm sure it had to do with math and whatever. But who has the time to figure this stuff out? Shouldn't we be spending all that brainpower curing cancer or something useful?

I shrugged. "I mean, it doesn't really affect me if lightning is hotter than the sun. I never got into those hypothetical questions."

"It's not hypothetical; it's a scientific fact," Shelby corrected me.

"Not a fact that I need to know. It's like, which came first, the chicken or the egg?"

"The chicken," Michael and Shelby responded in unison, each looking surprised at the other by their answer.

I laughed. "Oh, come on, really? How would you know that?"

"A chicken has a protein necessary for the formation of an egg; therefore an egg could only exist if it's been created by a chicken," Shelby stated as if it was obvious.

"Okaaay. Is that thing almost done?" I asked, trying to move on from the Michael and Shelby Holmes Random Scientific Knowledge Show.

"Almost." Shelby started to fill the cardboard from a toilet paper roll with the mixture.

"Well, good luck, with whatever that thing is," Michael replied. Then he looked at me. "And dealing with *him*."

Yeah, because *I* was the weirdo in this scenario.

Shelby put the finishing touches on the smoke bomb by placing a cardboard disk on top of the roll and inserting a fuse. Once she was satisfied, she put it in a paper bag and set it in the refrigerator with a sign that stated in large letters, "DO NOT TOUCH: PROPERTY OF SHELBY HOLMES."

"Explain it to me again? Do I really need to do this?" I tried to not whine, but this all made me a little uncomfortable.

"The critical piece of information we need in order to successfully retrieve Mr. Crosby's watch is the location of Ms. Semple's safe. We need Ms. Semple to think there's a fire so I can figure out where the safe is."

"Okay . . ." She had explained this to me before, but I still didn't understand how a fire—sorry, the *appearance* of fire—was going to help.

"When a mother hears a fire alarm, the first thing she does is go for her children, right?" I nodded. "Well, Mr. Crosby's watch is valuable to Ms. Semple. Therefore, if she thinks there's a fire, she'll most certainly think of it, and her other valuables in her safe, when she sees the smoke."

"And hears the alarm," I reminded her of the other part of my task for tomorrow.

"Right. But remember it's technically not the school alarm. You aren't tripping anything. *That* would be illegal. We're simply going to make Ms. Semple *think* there's a fire."

That was true. I was only pressing a button on Shelby's phone, hooked up to a speaker that would be outside Ms. Semple's office window, to simulate an alarm. Shelby had done research to figure out the exact make, model, and sound of the alarm system at Miss Adler's School. She then replicated it with her computer, recorded it, and had it on her phone.

"So when I get the signal, I light the smoke bomb and then press the button."

(Yeah, there was no way I wasn't getting caught.)

"It's a rather easy task."

"I don't see how we're going to get away with this." I made sure to say *we*, because if I was going down, I was taking Shelby with me.

"A few seconds. That's all I need. Just enough time to see Ms. Semple's initial reaction upon hearing the alarm and seeing the smoke. Then all will become clear. If we do everything as I've planned, nobody else in the school will even be aware of the pandemonium that will surely be ensuing in Ms. Semple's office. And in the chaos, I'll be able to quickly crack the safe, and then slip out with the watch in my possession."

I put my head in my hands. I started to feel throbbing in my temple. Yeah, I wanted some more adventure in my life, but maybe this was too much.

"Watson." Shelby placed her hand on my shoulder. "I

would never let anything happen to you. You know that, right?"

I looked up at her. Her face, which was usually scowling, was almost soft. She really was concerned about me.

"Yes."

"And you're with me on this, right? We need to help Mr. Crosby."

I nodded. I really liked Mr. Crosby. I didn't want to let him down.

"Believe me, if I could trade places with you I would," Shelby said. "But as much as I pride myself on being a master of disguise, I don't really see how I could transform you into a girl. So it has to be me in there, and you outside."

"I know," I replied. And I did. It wasn't that her plan didn't make sense. It was just . . . smoke. Fake fire. It seemed like so much could go wrong.

"The most danger we'll face is if Ms. Semple discovers who I am, but that'll never happen. Then after we're done, we'll meet at our rendezvous point and you'll simply have to try to blend in."

Honestly, that might be the hardest part. We're going to be at a swanky, all-girls' school on the Upper East Side. I'm a boy. I'm black. I looked down at myself. "I think it's going to be pretty hard for me to not stand out, Shelby."

She studied me for a moment before a smile spread on

her face. There was something about that smile that made me want to run the other way. Shelby rarely smiled, but if she did it meant one thing: trouble.

"Yes, you have a valid point, Watson. It's come to that juncture in the case where we focus on *your* wardrobe."

# ⌐•CHAPTER•⌐
# 16

"OH, JOHN, YOU LOOK SO NICE," MOM SAID ON Monday morning when I came out of my room wearing a white button-down shirt with a tie. And pressed khaki pants. This was the only outfit Shelby found suitable after she raided my closet last night. "All this for the museum?"

I should've known she would find this suspicious. I always complained when I had to wear nice clothes for church or holidays.

"Shelby thought I should dress up for the occasion." I found myself regurgitating Shelby's line when I asked her what I would say if anybody saw me dressed like this, on a day off from school, no less.

"Did she?" Mom asked with a raised eyebrow. "I'm surprised

you aren't hanging out with the guys today. You should have them over one of these days."

Mom met the guys at a school open house the first week of school. She was happy to see that I had made friends so quickly.

"Yeah. I will," I replied. I grabbed a piece of toast with peanut butter.

"What time are you leaving?"

"Soon," I replied as I took a big bite of toast. I had to be out front in five minutes to keep to our schedule.

"That's awfully early, isn't it? I thought most museums didn't open until ten."

I stopped chewing. It was currently 7:24 in the morning. I tried to think of yet another lie she'd believe.

"Shelby wanted to give me a proper tour of Central Park first."

Mom studied me for a second. I tried to look natural so she couldn't smell the deceit. "Well, I guess I should be happy you're spending your day off getting an education."

*She bought it!*

"I have to get to the hospital. Have a great day. And be careful." She gave me a quick kiss before grabbing her bag and leaving. I waited two minutes before heading out.

The hallway was clear. But when I opened the front door to our building, I froze. Mom was deep in conversation with Shelby. Yet she didn't know it.

"John, have you met Mrs. Hudson's niece, Basia?"

Shelby was in full undercover mode. She had told me that she would be in character on the bus ride over since you never knew who would be following us.

"Ah, yeah, hey," I stumbled over my words. "Nice to see you, Basia."

"Yes, my auntie already introduced us." Shelby, or Basia Rathbone, was dressed up like the other day. "John, I hope you don't mind if I accompany you and Shelby today on your trip to the museum."

"Cool," I responded. Every word was difficult to speak since my voice was shaking. We were so close to being caught. Shelby looked as unaffected as ever. But why *would* she be as freaked out as me? Nothing would happen to *her* if Mom knew who she really was. I, on the other hand, would be in so much trouble for the growing number of lies I'd told.

"Well, have a great day, you two," Mom said with a wave before heading to the subway.

I waited until she turned the corner onto Lenox Avenue before I exhaled with relief.

"We should get going, Watson," Shelby said in her sweet Basia voice. She slung a fancy messenger bag over her shoulder and then picked up her ratty, purple backpack that was beside her feet and handed it to me. "I am entrusting you with this today. I think it goes without saying that you need to be careful with it."

I took it by the handle. It had to weigh at least fifty pounds. "Whoa. How can you lug this thing around all the time?" I put it on as we headed to the bus stop.

"It has everything required to be a good detective. It's important to be prepared."

True, that backpack always seemed to have whatever Shelby needed when we were on a case: measuring tape, binoculars, magnifying glass, tape, tweezers, makeup (to dust for fingerprints), pretty much anything you can think of. Oh, yeah, and it currently held two smoke bombs (in case one didn't work).

Once we boarded our bus, Shelby leaned into me to whisper, "When we get off at our stop, follow behind me, but don't make it obvious. Sit down at the bench and read the book I brought for you. Wait precisely twelve minutes after the bell rings, then go to the window I told you about. There's plenty of room for you to stand underneath it without being seen. Wait for the signal."

"Got it." I unzipped her backpack, looking to see what book she had for me to read. And groaned at the sight of a ginormous chemistry book. "You want me to do homework?"

Seriously? Today was a *day off from school.*

"No. However, I presume that nobody would think that a smartly dressed young gentleman reading a huge textbook would be up to trouble."

Fair enough.

I leaned back on my seat as the bus drove through Central Park. I was still in awe of the city. Anytime I saw the Empire State Building peek up from behind buildings in Midtown, I still got chills. I doubted I'd ever be bored by Manhattan.

Shelby pressed the STOP strip, signaling the bus driver for the next stop, Fifth Avenue. We both exited, but I remained a few paces behind Shelby as instructed, looking over at the park every once in a while. When we got to the school, there were girls filing into the building. A girl with long black hair in a high ponytail and an olive complexion approached Shelby to greet her. Well, she greeted Basia.

"You must be Basia. Welcome to Miss Adler's School for Girls. We're so happy to have you here," the girl said in the same sweet tone Shelby had been imitating. Was this the official voice of the rich and privileged on the Upper East Side? "I'm Moira and I'll be showing you around today."

I kept walking over to the other side of the building, sat on a bench that faced the school, and opened up the textbook. Inside it were tons of notes that Shelby had taken about different kinds of chemical reactions. No wonder she knew how to make a smoke bomb off the top of her head.

I stole a glance to see Shelby still talking to the Moira girl. Before they walked in, Moira turned around and made eye contact with me. I quickly looked down at my book.

I tried to tell myself that she was simply looking around and seeing some black kid reading a huge chemistry book on a bench who did, in fact, stand out. But I couldn't shake the feeling that she was actually looking for me.

# CHAPTER 17

*DON'T STAND OUT. DON'T STAND OUT.*

I kept repeating that in my head as I placed the watch that was synced with Shelby's in the spine of the chemistry book. I took a chance and looked up to survey the area. Not one single person was paying any attention to me.

Maybe this undercover business wasn't so hard.

As there were only a few minutes left until class started, the line of black SUVs and a few limos started to thin out as the girls made their way inside the school that was built like a stone castle. It even had a turret, which made it different from the rows of town houses and apartment buildings that lined Fifth Avenue.

I studied the girls, some who were dropped off by nannies, a few by maids in uniforms, and one was even escorted by a dude who looked like a butler, top hat and all. I observed that the girls were all giggling, and well . . . *girly* until they approached the school. Then they all straightened their posture and started to behave like the prim and proper girls Shelby had been imitating all morning.

My mind wandered to what Shelby would be doing right now. She was probably biting her tongue because someone didn't have a fact right, or forcing a smile as someone droned on and on about a story that she didn't find educational.

It must be driving her nuts.

Oh, how I wished I could be a fly on that wall.

By the time the school bell rang at 8:30 sharp, the front was completely empty. The only people on the street were adults in business suits on their way to work. At precisely 8:42, I walked around the corner to the window that Shelby had assured me was in the headmistress's office. And true to her word, I could stand underneath it without being seen. I casually put the smoke bomb on the sidewalk and used my feet and bag to conceal it. I shoved the phone and speaker to sound the faux-alarm in my pocket and waited for my signal.

I wasn't exactly sure how Shelby was going to get the headmistress to open the window, but if I've learned anything from working with her, it was to never underestimate Shelby Holmes.

Less than a minute later I heard the window open above me. My heart skipped a beat. I could faintly hear Shelby's sugary voice, "Thank you so much. I have no idea what came over me. How horribly embarrassing."

The window was open. That was my cue.

I lit the fuse of the smoke bomb and hit the fake alarm. The smoke bomb began to emit a ton of white smoke, which blew directly into the open window because of the wind.

I held my breath and prayed that this would not be the one time that Shelby Holmes was wrong.

# CHAPTER 18

My heart was racing as I waited for Shelby on the corner of Madison and 74th, our designated meeting spot.

When I spotted her approaching, she was strolling casually like it was a Sunday afternoon, she didn't have anywhere to be, and, oh yeah, she didn't just steal something.

Well, she didn't just steal something *back*.

I was practically jumping out of my skin. "Did you get it?"

She paused, and a confident smile widened on her face. Even though she still had on her Basia Rathbone costume, every mannerism was pure Shelby Holmes. She reached into her bag and pulled out a watch. She twirled it around her finger. "It should go without saying that I would acquire our item."

"How'd you do it?" I asked.

"By sticking to our plan," she replied as she started walking down the block. "Put thought into a plan and come up with every possible scenario, and you'll be successful, Watson."

"Come on, Shelby," I prodded her. "Tell me what happened!" She usually relished telling people how brilliant she was to pull something off.

"Old news," Shelby replied with a wave of her hand.

"Yeah, well, won't I learn more if you tell me how you got the watch?"

"You make a valid point. I should take every opportunity to educate you." Shelby took a quick glance at the watch before putting it back into her bag. "After receiving a tour of the grounds from Moira, a seventh grader, I was escorted to Ms. Semple's office. As the interview commenced, I tried to pinpoint the various locations Ms. Semple could hide a safe. Behind framed art on the wall and in her desk were the most obvious places. Of course as I looked around, Ms. Semple assumed I was simply in awe of my surroundings: the plush, rich furniture, the large paintings of former headmistresses, and the antiques that adorned her office.

"It should go without saying that I piled on the charm that's expected of a young lady at Miss Adler's School. I began regaling Ms. Semple with stories of my studies abroad in London, which were fictional of course, but my commitment to details made her believe every word. Attention must always be paid to the minutiae if you wish to get away with even the simplest ruse. I heaped on declarations of my desire to become an Adler lady. Ms. Semple, in turn, was eating it up.

"As soon as I knew that there was more than adequate time for you to take your place, I started fanning myself. 'My goodness,' I said. 'My apologies, but I'm feeling a tad flush. It must be all this excitement of even the thought that I'd be fortunate enough to attend this fine institution.'" Shelby's face looked disgusted at the mere thought of attending Miss Adler's again.

"Ms. Semple offered to call the nurse, but instead I asked her to open the window, which she did. I must mention that I had no doubt you'd be there, Watson. After the window was open I let her know I was fine, which turned her attention to me again. I needed her focus to be on me so I could see where her eyes went when the smoke appeared. Once you sounded the alarm and the smoke came in, she looked across the room at a painting on the wall. And that was all I needed.

"I suggested that we exit the building. While Ms. Semple hesitated for a quick moment, she soon followed me through her office door, where there was no smoke to be seen or alarm to be heard. Ms. Semple's secretary was typing away on her computer and was utterly perplexed when Ms. Semple started inquiring about a fire."

"But how did you get back inside her office?"

Shelby grunted, aggravated that I'd interrupted her. "I'm

getting to that. You were the one who wanted details, Watson. *As I was saying,* I had purposefully left my bag inside Ms. Semple's office, so I pretended to remember it, and ducked in while Ms. Semple and her secretary were trying to figure out what was going on. I quickly removed the painting and found a safe behind it. I have to say, I was very underwhelmed by the lock. It was simple. I pulled out the tools that I had hidden under my skirt, and it took me no more than twenty seconds to open the safe. The watch was on top of a bunch of documents. I took the watch, closed the safe, put the painting back in place, and grabbed my bag.

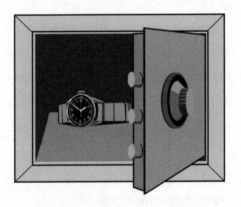

"When I walked out of her office, Ms. Semple was on the phone with maintenance, trying to figure out if there was a faulty alarm. She was preoccupied, so I simply slipped away. As far as they know, Basia Rathbone decided to study elsewhere."

It all really had gone according to her plan. Every single

detail had been figured out, and executed flawlessly. I was almost disappointed it was over. But not really, since it wasn't even 9:30 and that meant I had enough time to go home, change out of these stuffy clothes, and get to Rucker Park to play ball with the guys.

John Watson: detective, friend, *and* athlete.

"So we're done?" I asked.

"Yes," Shelby replied with an uninterested sniff. "Mr. Crosby has been notified that I'm in possession of his watch. I'll be meeting him later today. Then he can let Lestrade know about Ms. Semple's failed blackmail and our successful retrieval. You've done quite well for yourself, Watson. I truly couldn't have done this without you."

"Thanks, Shelby!" All the stress of the last couple days had disappeared. Instead I was excited that we solved yet another case. We came through for Mr. Crosby. Plus, I was going to have an awesome journal entry out of this. I was becoming better each day with all this sleuthing stuff.

We turned the corner and stopped.

There, blocking our way with her arms folded and a triumphant smile on her face, was the girl from outside the school. The one who gave Shelby the tour. The one who I thought was looking for me.

"Hello, *Basia.*"

What was she doing here? Were we caught? What happened to us if we were?

In a flash, Shelby transformed back into her prep school character. "Why, hello, Moira. Thank you again for an absolutely delightful tour of the school. This is an old friend from my previous school, Bruce Nigels." It amazed me how quickly Shelby could come up with an alias. "Bruce, this is Moira."

"Hello," I said in an overly deep voice as I extended my hand, but in a wooden, less natural way. I figured if Bruce was friends with someone like Basia, he probably was a bit of a bore. "Pleasure."

"I'm surprised to see you, Moira. Not that it isn't a wonderful surprise." Shelby (well, Basia) didn't seem to be worried, but that didn't mean much. It was usually pretty impossible to read Shelby, even when she was being herself.

"Yes," Moira said as she flipped her ponytail. "I believe you were looking for this." She reached into her blue school blazer pocket and pulled out a watch.

My mouth fell open while Shelby didn't move a muscle. (So much for me being cool undercover.)

"What's that?" Shelby asked in such a sweet voice, I almost believed she was clueless.

Moira tsked. "You know exactly what it is. I'm disappointed that you didn't inspect the watch in the safe to make sure it was Mr. Crosby's. What you have in your possession is a replica of the Bulova A-17, the successor to the A-11. But never once did you think to check. Your ego does get in the way, doesn't it?"

*Ouch.* But still no reaction from Shelby.

"Did you really think Ms. Semple was behind this?" Moira continued. "She's about as useless as it comes. A kindergartener could've hacked into her e-mail and broken into her safe, as you've proven, *Basia.* Did you think I was going to leave the real watch in the safe? That I was going to make this easy for you?"

*Easy*?! She thought THAT was *easy*?

And if Moira had Mr. Crosby's watch, what did we have?

Oh, and you know, WHO WAS THIS GIRL AND WHY WOULD SHE DO THIS?

I remained mute as I waited for Shelby to respond. She was still in Basia mode: perfect posture, wide eyes, and pleasant smile on her face. She looked Moira up and down.

Okay, Shelby was going to figure this out. She would know what to do.

"I think it would be extremely helpful if you could answer a question for me," Shelby said, although usually when Shelby asked a question, she already knew the answer.

"Please," Moira responded with a crooked smile.

"What exactly do you want with Mr. Crosby?"

*Okay! Good! Figure out what she wants so we can give it to her, get the real watch, and then get out of here.*

"This has absolutely nothing to do with Mr. Crosby." A smile started to spread on Moira's lips. "Imagine my delight when I realized that my naive former teacher was the best way for me to set everything in motion. Because what I really wanted was to see your face when you realized you failed, Shelby Holmes."

# CHAPTER 19

*OH NO.*

*No. No. NO. NO!*

How on earth did Moira figure out who Shelby was when even *I* was fooled by Basia Rathbone when I first met her?

I was staring at Shelby, waiting to see what she was going to do.

In a flash, Shelby hunched over in her usual sloppy posture, and her scowl returned. Actually, it was more of a sneer. I've never seen Shelby angry. (Extremely displeased and annoyed? Yes. Oh yes. But angry? No.) To be honest, as long as it wasn't directed at me, I was curious what was going to happen.

"So let's dispense with this farce, shall we?" Moira said. Then to my horror, she turned to me. "Don't you agree, John Watson?"

She knew who *I* was? How did she know me? Nobody knew me. I wasn't a local legend like Shelby.

"I, er, I," I stuttered. (Yep, nothing legendary about me.)

"Well," Shelby said, taking charge, "if we're to start dispensing the truth, then tell me what you want so we can get on with this."

Moira took the watch and put it back in the inside pocket of her blazer. "You don't remember me?"

Shelby yawned. An actual yawn. "I only remember people of significance."

Moira clenched her jaw. "Shelby Holmes, as self-important as ever. To be honest, I had forgotten all about you until your name started popping up recently. *The Great Shelby Holmes*," Moira said with spite. "The pint-sized detective who solves crimes. Honestly, I find your methods a bit pedestrian."

*Uh-oh.* I braced myself, ready to pull Shelby off Moira if I needed to. You didn't mess with Shelby. She studied jujitsu.

Shelby rolled her eyes. "Yes, clearly you went through all this trouble because you're utterly unimpressed by me. Envy doesn't look good on anybody, Moira."

"Why would I be jealous of somebody who failed their teacher? You couldn't perform the simple task of retrieving a beloved family heirloom. I'm very curious about how you're going to write about this in your online journal, Watson."

Shelby glared at me.

(Was it wrong that I was kinda excited that Moira had read my writing? I mean, it's cool that it was gaining a readership.

Although . . . it might have gotten us into this mess.)

Moira continued, "Perhaps you should change the name of your journal from *The Great Shelby Holmes* to *The Sometimes Satisfactory Shelby Holmes*." Moira laughed lightly, and then turned it into a sigh. "Well, it's been such a . . . hmm. My manners dictate that I say it's been a pleasure. Yet the truth is that I'm a little disappointed in our reunion." Moira shook her head as she turned to walk away.

"Wait!" I called after her. It can't end like this. We came too close. "Fine! You got us! Happy?"

I could hear Shelby grinding her teeth next to me, no doubt appalled that I would admit defeat. But forget pride, we needed that watch.

"What do you want?" I asked again. Everybody had a price. There was no way she went through all of this solely to rub it in our faces.

Moira turned around with a satisfied look on her face. "I don't want anything from you. Seeing you fail miserably has been reward enough. Proving that I am, in fact, better than you was all I needed. You can assure Mr. Crosby that his favorite former student, Moira Hardy, was able to safely retrieve his watch and that it will be returned to him shortly.

Although I am tempted to keep it. It would be a lovely memento of defeating you."

"Day's not over yet," Shelby replied confidently.

Moira laughed again. It was extremely aggravating. "Well, when I return to Miss Adler's, in addition to educating Ms. Semple on your true identity, I'll make sure the security guards know to not allow you access." Moira began to walk away.

"Good luck," Shelby replied. Moira turned around with an eyebrow raised. "Ms. Semple wants me to return to Miss Adler's. If she finds out Basia's true identity, she'll be running around the streets looking for me. She'll *beg* me to come back into the building."

"She doesn't want you at Miss Adler's. That was all part of my charade."

"Oh, really? For the last two years, *you've* been writing me letters asking me to return?"

Moira scowled. "While you may have Ms. Semple fooled, I'm regarded as an exemplary student at Miss Adler's. My name holds weight. If I say you're out, you're out. End of story. I know being a bigger person isn't something you're usually capable of, but perhaps you should just admit defeat before you trouble yourself any further."

Shelby straightened up so she was closer to eye level with Moira (although Shelby was still several inches shorter). "It's no trouble at all, really."

"Famous last words," Moira sang out as she walked away with a skip in her step. She turned the corner and vanished from our sight.

"What was that all about?" I asked. I mean, REALLY?

Shelby reached into her bag and pulled out the watch. She studied it before throwing it down on the ground and stomping on it.

"It's a fake. I can't believe it. I didn't examine it, Watson." Shelby's face was pinched in anger. "I was . . . careless." She leaned against the brick wall of a storefront in shock.

That made two of us.

Shelby didn't make mistakes. She had assumed the watch she found was the right one. Why wouldn't it be? I had so many questions. "So Ms. Semple had nothing to do with it?"

"No. Moira used her as a front. Mr. Crosby never would've taken threats from a former student seriously. My initial hunches were correct that this was out of character for Ms. Semple. Mr. Crosby was never e-mailing with Ms. Semple; it was Moira the entire time."

Yeah, Shelby had thought it didn't seem like something Ms. Semple would do. Of course *I* thought the *whole thing* was fishy all along! I knew a headmistress wouldn't go through all of that to get a student back. Which led to the most pressing question.

"Why would Moira do this? I don't get it."

"Moira is a rich girl with too much time on her hands. She's proven to be a slight nuisance, but nothing we can't handle."

*We.* I still got a surge of pride when Shelby included me (and not only when she needed me to set off a smoke bomb).

"You really don't remember her? You must've gone to school with her when you were at Miss Adler's."

Shelby looked thoughtful for a moment. "I'm aware of her surname because it's on many plaques throughout the school, as the Hardy family is one of the main benefactors of the school. But I do not remember Moira from my time there. She does seem familiar, but not from a few years ago. I've seen her more recently." Shelby closed her eyes, and her lips began to move as she tried to place Moira. It was something I'd seen her do before when she tried to access information in her brain attic.

After a few minutes, she opened her eyes.

"Anything?" I asked.

"Not yet. But even if I could remember her, it still leaves us without a watch."

"Moira said she was going to return it to Mr. Crosby."

Shelby scoffed. "Oh, Watson, I'm not going to let her best me."

I didn't think anybody could best Shelby. But maybe she had met her match? Moira seemed to be a step ahead of us.

"Maybe we should. Mr. Crosby gets his watch, while we can chalk this up as a learning experience." I wasn't sure what we had to learn except that Moira Hardy had some serious jealousy issues.

"We will not be defeated, Watson," Shelby stated with her hands on her hips. "While my mind may have been clouded with Moira's traps and using Ms. Semple as her cover, I am seeing clearly now."

"But what can we do?"

"We are going to get that watch! We will not let Mr. Crosby down. Plus, Moira needs to know that she can't mess with Shelby Holmes and John Watson."

Shelby's confidence was contagious. She was right: Who did this Moira think we were? We didn't give up! We were going to fix this!

Basketball with the guys was a million miles away. All that mattered now was seeing this case through to the end.

"You're right!" I said as I pumped my fist into the air.

"Of course I am," Shelby stated matter-of-factly. "You know what we have to do."

"We're going after her," I said, more as a statement than a question.

"Affirmative." Shelby's eyes were focused on the corner where Moira disappeared. "Let's go."

# CHAPTER 20

"Stay close," Shelby instructed as we walked straight, instead of turning at the same corner as Moira.

"I thought we were following her."

"There's no need to follow when we know her next location. It's better that we stay out of sight. For now."

Ah, right. Moira was going back to school.

"Do you really not remember her from when you were in school together?" I pressed. Shelby remembered everything. I had a feeling she was keeping something from me.

"No, I do not, Watson," she snapped. "I realize this is yet another mental error on my part, and I do not need you reminding me of it. I threw out the bulk of my Miss Adler's brain files a while ago. Honestly, I didn't expect the students there to be of any importance for a future case."

"But you must've done something to make her mad."

Shelby scowled at me. "If being the smartest person in school at age six can make somebody mad, then yes, she probably was mad at me. She can get in line behind all the students at the Academy who take issue with my intelligence."

Of course I was on Shelby's side, but . . . if Moira had been holding a grudge all this time, I could see why. It was pretty hard not to find Shelby grating and condescending sometimes.

And I'm speaking as her closest (and only) friend.

We reached the edge of Central Park where we could easily see the school. We stood on the other side of the stone wall that bordered the park.

Shelby looked out at Miss Adler's. "Let's examine what we know about Moira: she's rich, jealous, and, most troublesome, extremely clever. There wasn't much to deduce from her appearance since her school uniform was pristine: a marker of having a maid. Her hair was also incredibly tidy; not a single strand was out of place. A clue that perhaps someone did her hair for her. It could possibly be her mother, but Moira's family has a lot of money so her parents probably don't spend a lot of time with her. She's surrounded by people who are paid to take care of her."

"You can tell that by her clothes and hair?"

"I can tell you have a busy working mother by your clothes."

I looked down at the nicest outfit I had. "Oh, come on, you can't tell that by—"

Shelby lifted my arm and turned it so the buttons of my cuff were showing. "You're missing a button. It's nothing really, but it shows me that your caretaker doesn't have the time, nor the proclivity, to find a matching button to sew on."

Okay, even though she was right, Shelby knew my mom. She knew the hours she worked as a doctor. Plus, there were two other buttons, so who cared if the middle one was missing?

Oh, that's right. *Shelby Holmes* cared about every tiny detail. "It's just a shirt."

"Exactly, Watson!" Shelby exclaimed. "It's only clothes. To you and me. Moira lives in a different world. Everybody at her school, and I venture to deduce in her world, has a great deal of money. Appearances are everything. Her parents have to have the best-dressed child, the *smartest* child . . ."

"But the Lacys weren't that way." The Lacys were my only guide into the world of the wealthy.

"Oh, Tamra would be considered a scholarship student at Miss Adler's," Shelby replied with a laugh.

*Are you kidding me?* The Lacys had that ridiculous apartment and a private driver and chef and maid and . . . They had *everything*.

"As I said, this is a different world."

"Is that why you left?" I asked, because I couldn't imagine

Shelby fitting in with all those girls I saw walking into the school that morning. Not like she could fit in many places, but still. "Did you like it there?"

Shelby shrugged. "I had wrongly assumed with all of their monetary resources, I'd be given the best education possible. Unfortunately, the students were more concerned with who vacationed where and what country they were going to visit next. If any of them even deigned to acknowledge the scholarship kid, they made fun of me. Which would have been okay if they could've come up with anything clever besides throwing around the predictable 'poor' and 'nerd' insults. That's why I like the Academy. We're all poor and middle-class nerds there. Well, not all of us. There are the Tamras, but she's the exception to the rule."

It sounded like Miss Adler's was a hard place to make friends. I didn't think it was possible, but I started feeling a little sorry for Moira. "So she's hung up on the fact that you were the best student?"

"At this juncture, it appears that could be her motive. It's obvious she's jealous of me, and your online reporting has certainly set off a spark."

Yikes. I never thought my online posts would ever ruin a case for us. But, hey, at least I had a new reader!

"Have *you* read my journal?"

"I don't need to read what I've lived."

"Oh, okay." I tried to not let her know that bummed me out.

"But I'm sure it's adequate, Watson."

*Gee, thanks.*

"Did you learn anything about Moira during your tour?"

"Besides the fact that she's an incompetent guide? She was off by a year on the date Miss Adler's was founded *and* that there are three, not two, Pulitzer Prize–winning alumni. Yes, there was one other thing, which is why I've returned us here. On my tour I played the role of the guileless prospective student to a T, so I asked her about the cafeteria. Moira told me that she goes home for lunch. So we're going to wait until she walks home, then we'll ambush her and get the watch. Plain and simple."

Was it really going to be that easy?

"What if it's a trap? You said she's smart, so what if she's anticipating that we'll follow her?"

"Excellent point, Watson! Moira has proven to be a very calculating person, so there is a possibility she told me that fact on purpose." Shelby seemed weirdly impressed that Moira could be setting a trap. "If it's a game she wants, we'll play it. Either way, we'll get that watch."

"But what if she's expecting us?"

"We must remain vigilant." Shelby glanced at her watch. "We have some time before lunch, and there's no point in keeping up appearances." She took off her wig, then shook out her hair, which was messier than usual (which was saying *a lot*). Then, to my horror, she pulled her skirt down.

"Shelby!" I yelped before realizing she had a pair of shorts on under her skirt.

"Relax, Watson. You can be so uptight." Shelby removed her cardigan and put it in her backpack. Then she took off her patent leather shoes and replaced them with a beat-up pair of sneakers.

I loosened my tie and unbuttoned the top button of my shirt. "You don't happen to have a T-shirt in there for me, do you?"

"Certainly not."

Hey, it didn't hurt to ask. I removed my tie and rolled up my sleeves since it was pretty warm for late September.

As we sat waiting, I thought about how Shelby described the students there. How they picked on her. I kept circling back to the fact that Moira would be going home for lunch. I'm sure Miss Adler's had a pretty decent cafeteria. She was definitely setting up a trap or . . .

"What is it?" Shelby asked. She could always tell when I was figuring something out.

"What's the food like at Miss Adler's?"

"It was adequate. However, they insisted on serving you

both a fruit and vegetable, all organic, of course, and the dessert portion was sorely lacking."

I had a feeling the food was awesome.

"Okay, desserts aside, would you go home for lunch if your house was across the street from school?"

"Yes," Shelby replied immediately. "Then I could get some peace and quiet instead of having to block out the incessant babbling in the cafeteria."

"Okay, but I wouldn't. Lunch is when I can chill and talk to my friends. There would only be one reason that I wouldn't want to eat lunch at school."

"The food?"

"No. Shelby, I don't think Moira has any friends. Or at least she isn't well liked."

"It goes without saying that she isn't well liked, Watson. You've met her, haven't you?" she asked with a snort.

Point taken.

"What does that have to do with anything?" Shelby took out a candy bar and began devouring it.

I knew I had to proceed with caution. Shelby didn't really see the point of having friends so I didn't want to offend her.

"I'm simply making an observation about her character. Isn't that what you always tell me to do? Moira's probably really lonely. Why else would she put all this effort into . . . I don't know . . . hacking a headmistress's e-mail and stealing a former teacher's watch. And that's just two of the things she's done. That we know of."

I couldn't imagine someone who was happy causing all this trouble.

Shelby looked thoughtful for a moment while she chewed on her second candy bar. "You've made a valid observation about Moira, Watson. It's always smart to get inside an enemy's mind. She's someone who managed this complex plan solely to best us. She had to hack into Ms. Semple's e-mail, steal Mr. Crosby's watch, and then break into Ms. Semple's safe to put a different watch there for us to steal. What's most, dare I say, impressive is that she had anticipated our moves. She knew I would disguise myself to get to the watch."

"How?" I asked, still trying to wrap my brain around it all. I'd thought Shelby was the only person smart enough to come up with our plan. Moira not only had her own plan, but she also knew what our moves would be and was always one step ahead.

Shelby looked at the school, her face scrunched up more than normal. "I really don't know, Watson."

Okay, I was officially freaked. I always thought that I'd enjoy it when Shelby was clueless about something, but we needed her to figure this out. And fast.

We waited outside, mostly in silence, for nearly two hours until the school's lunch break at 12:15. The whole time we were waiting, we never moved more than a foot from our hiding spot.

My stomach was grumbling. I'd become used to eating lunch at 11:15 at school. Plus, I was so stressed when Mom was grilling me this morning that I didn't even finish my toast. Right as I was about to ask Shelby if I could run and get a snack, she pulled me into a crouch. "There she is."

Moira walked down the steps of the school as her eyes swept in every direction, presumably looking for us. We squatted behind the stone wall, our faces partially obscured so she couldn't see us.

Or she could, but wasn't letting on.

"Shelby, I have a bad feeling about this." I knew that we needed to finish our assignment. I really did. And I couldn't wait to see the look on Moira's face when we got our hands on that watch. But there was this feeling in my gut that I couldn't ignore. Shelby knew everything, but she didn't know what Moira wanted with us, or what was in store once we cornered her.

"You're overreacting, Watson. Try to be reasonable: What's the worst that could happen? We don't get the watch. Well, we don't have it now. At the very least, we need to try."

One of the many differences between me and Shelby was that she was always practical, while I had an imagination. And right then, there were a million scenarios going through my head.

And all of them were worst case.

# CHAPTER 21

THERE ARE OVER 1.6 MILLION PEOPLE WHO LIVE IN THE borough of Manhattan. And that doesn't take into account the tourists or the people who commute here for work.

So you'd expect every street to be swarming with people. And most of the time that's true. Up in Harlem, 125th Street is full of tourists and street vendors. The avenues are usually busy, too, but sometimes you get that random side street that's weirdly empty.

And that's exactly what was happening on East 73rd Street. It was deserted. There was nobody to hide behind, leaving Shelby and me in plain sight if Moira were to look behind her. Shelby dragged me around the corner so we were hidden on Fifth Avenue.

"I have a better idea," Shelby said as she reached into her bag and pulled out her phone. She began typing angrily. I stared at her. Shelby *never* looked up things on her phone. She just knew stuff.

"Okay, I know where she lives," Shelby said. "We're going to go around her, but we need to be fast." She then began running down Fifth Avenue, toward 72nd Street.

Now, I'm someone who's in fairly good shape. I play basketball, baseball, and can run a football, but what Shelby was doing was a full-on sprint. I quickly found myself nearly a half block behind her. The only time she paused was if the light was red. After an exhausting few minutes (it felt like twenty, but was more like four), we stopped on Park Avenue (well, she reached it and I got there about ninety seconds later).

"Okay," Shelby said. She wasn't out of breath, while I was wiping the sweat off my brow and on the verge of hyperventilating. "That's her building." She pointed to a fancy apartment building on the corner that did make the Lacys' look a little less impressive. "We're going to walk in and wait for her."

"What?" I snuck a glance at the building. "There's a doorman. How are we going to get by him? Are you going to put your Basia costume back on?"

"There's no time." Shelby handed me a tissue so I could wipe the sweat that was running down my face. "Plus, it's quite simple: we need to pretend that we belong there. People in the service industry, especially at a building with wealthy, entitled tenants, are trained to be extremely accommodating.

The last thing they want to do is offend a bratty rich kid. Follow my lead and try to catch your breath."

Shelby turned the corner and marched to the front door of the apartment building like she lived there.

"Let me tell you," she began in a very loud voice with a hint of a British accent, "I told Daddy that I was not going to tolerate a chef who couldn't make a proper beef Wellington. Can you even imagine?"

No, I couldn't imagine because I had no idea what she was talking about.

"It's so difficult to find good help, and we've already gone through four maids this month alone. I know we're new to town, but really?"

The doorman, who had on a long, emerald green blazer, was facing forward, but his eyes glanced over at Shelby. She stood right next to him. "Well?" she asked impatiently.

The guy gave her a friendly smile, "Can I help you, miss?"

"Correct me if I have this wrong, but it's your job to open the door, right? Must I do everything myself?"

The doorman's eyes nearly popped out of their sockets, stunned at how rude Shelby was being (I was as well, although I was more used to it than this poor guy). He hesitated for a moment, then Shelby pulled out her cell phone. "Daddy is going to love this."

"My apologies, Miss . . . ?" He tried to fish for her name as he opened the door.

Shelby let out an exasperated sigh as she walked into the marble lobby and ignored the guy behind the front desk. He started to talk to her, but then his eyes went to the front door and he stopped talking. The doorman was probably warning him. We walked toward the elevator banks, but then Shelby stepped to the left and had us hide in an alcove where the mailboxes were, and where we had a perfect view of the elevators.

Less than two minutes later, we heard the front desk attendant greet Moira. We had cut it close.

"Can you try to control your panting?" Shelby hissed at me. I *was* breathing hard. Wow, I was out of shape. My hands were also trembling slightly. It was way past my time to eat, and I was getting sluggish. I should've asked Shelby for a candy bar, since my blood sugar had to have been low.

I leaned against the wall and tried to calm myself down while Shelby peeked out to see where Moira was heading. I could hear the ding of the elevator and the doors open and close.

"Interesting," Shelby said with squinted eyes.

"What's interesting?"

"Moira's hand went to the up button when she went to call the elevator, but then she hesitated and pressed the down button instead. She went to the basement."

"So she's set a trap for us?"

"She's a very calculating person, but that slight pause

makes me think that perhaps she wasn't anticipating us coming here. Now she knows we did, and isn't confident about what to do."

"How would she know we're here?"

"It wouldn't surprise me if the doorman was agitated after letting us in. He must've given us away."

He wasn't the first person to be a little freaked out after running into Shelby.

"Let's go," Shelby said as she walked past the elevators. For a brief moment I thought we were leaving. But she kept walking and went through a door marked Stairs.

"Be very careful," Shelby whispered in the concrete stairway. "And quiet."

I followed Shelby down a flight of stairs. It was impressive how light she was on her feet. You couldn't hear her as she quickly descended the stairs, while I had to take each step slowly since my dress shoes had a hard heel.

When we finally got to the basement door, Shelby needed me to sneak a glance through its small rectangular window since she wasn't tall enough. I didn't like what I saw. Or more like what I didn't see. While the lobby was marble and fancy, the basement was concrete and dark. I could only see some pipes and a couple of doors. Moira wasn't there.

Shelby looked at me and furrowed her brow. "Are you feeling okay?"

I nodded, even though I'd felt better. I figured the sooner we got this over with, the sooner we could leave and be done with Moira. And eat. And get something to drink.

"You haven't eaten in five hours. That's late for you." Shelby started digging through her bag. "I've been so distracted I didn't realize your blood sugar must be low. I don't think I have anything in here."

"I'm fine," I assured her, even though I couldn't believe that the one time I needed sugar, Shelby was out.

"Maybe you should go upstairs and grab a juice somewhere? I can handle this myself."

While it was touching that Shelby was concerned about my health, I was more worried about what Moira would do.

"Shelby, I don't want you to be alone. The two of us can easily take care of Moira. Let's finish this," I replied.

Shelby slowly turned the knob of the door, and we made our way into the basement hallway. One of the doors was closed, the other open.

Shelby gave me a nod as we walked toward the open door and into whatever trap Moira had set up for us.

# ᕙ·CHAPTER·ᕗ
# 22

THE ROOM WAS A LARGE CONCRETE BOX WITH A HUGE canister taking up an entire wall and pipes snaking along the other three. It was dark, damp, and a little steamy.

There was a loud humming coming from the canister, but besides that constant noise it was quiet, except for the clacking of my shoes (as much as I tried to muffle them). Shelby immediately started scanning the room as we passed through the door. I squinted into the darkness, but couldn't see anything, or anybody.

Shelby turned around. "Hiding behind the door? Really?" she said with a snicker. "How truly unremarkable."

The air was sticky and silent. For a moment, I thought maybe Moira wasn't there. Okay, so I was kinda hoping she wouldn't be.

But after a few more beats, the door squeaked and Moira stepped out from behind it. "That's rather ironic, since I'm the one who finds herself consistently dissatisfied with you,

Shelby. Following me home for lunch? How predictable . . ." Moira clicked her tongue like she was scolding a small child. "Although everything has gone according to my plan thus far. Of course you'd do exactly what I wanted you to do."

The humidity in the room was unbearable. I thought I was sweating before, but now my clothes were almost soaked through. There was even sweat on both Moira's and Shelby's brows.

"I would assume that you'd be used to disappointments by now," Shelby replied with that smirk of hers. She had deduced something about Moira, and was going to let her have it. "Although I can understand it, with everything you've been through. I almost feel bad for you, Moira."

Oh, this was good. Here Moira thought she had trapped us, when it was the opposite. Shelby was setting her up for . . . something.

"*You* feel sorry for *me*?" Moira laughed. "Oh, that's precious. Thank you for the laugh, Shelby."

"I certainly do. Your cries for attention are practically deafening. Tell me, are you doing all of this to try to impress people at school since you don't have any friends?"

*Hey!* That came from me! I finally made a correct deduction. I had to be right for Shelby to use it. Although now I felt a little bad that it was being thrown in Moira's face.

Shelby wasn't done yet. "Or is this all a ploy to get your father's attention, since he'd rather be working than be home with you."

*Ouch.* Now I did feel sorry for Moira.

Shelby gave me a quick glance, probably knowing how much her comment might've hit home with me because of my relationship with my dad.

Shelby sucked in a breath. "I GOT IT!"

She did! What did she have?

Shelby folded her arms as a smile spread across her face. "How was your St. Bart's vacation with the Lacys?"

*WHAT*? Moira knew the Lacys? They went on vacation together? How on earth did Shelby figure that out?

Shelby wagged her finger at Moira. "I knew I'd seen you recently. Granted, it took me a while to put the pieces together. But you were in one of the photos on the Lacys' bureau. You, your parents, and the Lacys at a resort in St. Bart's. Last Christmas, I presume?"

Moira's jaw went slack.

Shelby was right! One of the clues to the Lacys' dognapping case had to do with a missing picture frame on a bureau in the upstairs hallway. I'd glanced at those photos when we were there, but I hadn't really observed. Part of me couldn't believe Shelby remembered those photos so clearly, but the other part of me was grateful she did. Because now we knew more about Moira.

Moira's eyes were glued on Shelby as she paced the room.

"Yes. Your family is friends with the Lacys. My impressive exploits no doubt came up through them. And you recalled being in school with me. How upsetting it must've been to be reminded of the first grader who came to your school and advanced a grade after only a month. Who was heaped with praise by all the teachers. I was put in a few of your classes, even though you're three years older than me.

Yet even though you were older, I knew more than you. Even then. That must've hurt. Being outsmarted. I wouldn't know. It's not a feeling I'm familiar with. And then a few years later, you had to listen to your parents gush about the abilities of the same brilliant young girl." Shelby then turned to Moira. "That really got to you. You're an only child, used to having all the attention. You'd become accustomed to being the smartest in class once more. And then I came along . . . again. Even now, when we're in different schools, you can't compete with me."

"You don't know what you're talking about," Moira replied, but the quiver in her voice said differently.

"Ah, yes, it's coming together. You needed to prove to yourself that you could beat me. How petty, how naive, how utterly unsuccessful. Oh, Moira, you may have money, but you don't have the talents."

"I fooled you!" Moira growled. "I did. I got the best of you. I have the watch!"

"You do, for now. But then what? You said you were going to return the watch to Mr. Crosby. Why even bring him into this?"

"Because when I found out he was now teaching at your school, I knew he was the way to get to you. That your ego couldn't resist swooping in to save the day."

Point Moira.

"Okay, so you return Mr. Crosby's watch. Then what?"

Moira began to stammer. "I—I—"

Shelby replied by mimicking Moira's tsking. "You haven't thought this all the way through, have you? Revenge can be a powerful motivator, but it also doesn't allow people to think clearly."

"Isn't that why *you're* here?" Moira asked as her eyes narrowed. "Revenge."

Shelby looked confused for a moment. "Not at all. You have to actually care about someone to want revenge. For me, this is simply about completing a task for a client. Let's get back to it. Yes, you knew my steps up until this morning. While that is impressive, you don't know what I'm going to do next."

So Moira and I had that in common, because I was also clueless.

Shelby looked like a lion that was circling its prey. "You never imagined we'd get this far. You thought your security desk was going to stop us. You planned on having a normal lunch, and if you saw us, you were going to have security swoop in to save the day. Once you realized we were in the building, you decided to bring us here. So I ask you again, Moira, now what?"

Moira was shaking with anger, her face red (although that could've been from the heat, but I was pretty sure it was from Shelby). "I bested you! I did!" Moira started stomping her feet. "*I* was the one who figured out a way to get you to come to me. *I* knew you'd find a way into Ms. Semple's office and do something to get her to reveal her hiding place. *I* gave her a very generous check from my father this morning to ensure that she would look at her safe. That was *me*. *I* did that. *I* was able to think one step ahead of you the whole time. You've been *my* puppet. *I* am the one pulling the strings. Everything has happened because I planned it. Not the great Shelby Holmes. Somebody needed to put you in your place, and I decided that person was me."

Moira started laughing like she had us. But she didn't.

Did she?

We were stuck in a basement. There was only one way out. There were two of us, and only one of Moira. And Moira was unraveling.

"We're more alike than you think," Moira said.

"You wish."

"I find school to be dreadfully boring. The people in the school, idiots. I have a restless mind. I know you do, too. So I knew that if I gave you a series of hoops to jump through, you'd be more than happy to do it. But I also realized that you'd be so distracted by these bizarre complications—blackmail, a stolen watch, Ms. Semple—that you'd never see me coming."

She had us there.

"Do you also find this conversation boring?" Shelby asked as she yawned.

Moira narrowed her eyes at Shelby. "You think you're so smart."

"I don't think I'm smart, I *know* I am," Shelby fired back. "Although I'm not so insecure that I require validation, so this ends now. You hand over the watch, or your sterling reputation at Miss Adler's is finished. After all, I don't think Ms. Semple would have any problem expelling you after she finds out you hacked her e-mail, blackmailed a former teacher, and threatened a beloved alumnus. But then again, you getting expelled would perhaps finally get you the attention from your family that you so desperately crave. Please let me know if you require an autograph as proof that you've met me."

"You're ... I don't need to ..." Moira was stumbling over her words. It was clear that Shelby had hit a big nerve. "Like you have a ton of friends and a perfect family."

Shelby laughed. "It goes without saying that nobody has a perfect family. However, we have the opposite problem, Moira. I don't *want* all the attention my parents try to heap on me. But that's how they show affection so it's difficult to argue against it. As for friends, well, I don't crave them. Watson suits me fine."

*Um, thanks?*

Moira's hands were balled into fists. I had a feeling that Shelby was making this worse. I couldn't imagine Moira simply handing over the watch now.

Maybe it was time to stop being mute and try to really reason with Moira, without threats or painful blows to her ego.

"All right," I said as I stepped between them. "It's time we think this through. Moira, you have something we want. If you hand it over now, we'll go on our way and you'll never see or hear from us again. We won't make any trouble. But if you don't, well . . . I can't be held responsible for what Shelby will do."

Okay, it was kinda nice to threaten her.

Moira rolled her eyes (it was a little eerie how much she had in common with Shelby in terms of her mannerisms). "I thought you were only here to protect Shelby, Watson. I didn't realize you actually *spoke*."

Shelby sneered. "I don't need protection."

Moira looked at Shelby's tiny stature and laughed.

Shelby took a step forward. "Would you like me to prove it to you?"

I reached around Shelby to hold her back. (Why was I protecting Moira from Shelby? Maybe I should let Shelby get a few karate kicks in.)

I was struggling to contain Shelby. I probably weighed fifty pounds more than her and could see over her head, but I felt weak. I wanted to blame the heat. And the fact that I was hungry. And thirsty. And suddenly really tired.

Moira took a step to the side so she was between the exit and us.

"Okay, fine. Yeah, I didn't think you'd find a way into my apartment building. Clearly, my father will be having a talk with security. But here you are. Well, Shelby and Watson, since you're such geniuses, good luck finding your way out." Moira walked through the door, slamming it shut behind her.

It was completely pitch black.

And we were locked in.

# CHAPTER 23

IT WAS SO DARK, I COULDN'T SEE ANYTHING. *ANYTHING.*

I heard Shelby fidgeting around, and then a beam of light appeared. Shelby pointed her flashlight in my face, I held up my hands to protect my eyes. "Are you okay?"

I nodded. "Yeah."

"You don't appear to be in optimal health."

"I'm fine," I assured her. "How are we going to get out of here?"

Shelby shone her light around the room. "My phone isn't getting any service. We'll have to make noise or, even better, break something so somebody has to come down to fix it."

"Why's it so hot?" I asked. I thought it was bad before, but now with the door closed there was no air in here except for disgusting damp . . . stuff. I couldn't even think straight anymore.

"We're in the boiler room. That boiler over there heats water and delivers it to all the apartment units." Shelby started banging on the pipes with a screwdriver from her bag. I know I should've offered to help, but I was feeling really out of it. "Usually it's not this hot," she continued, "but it's an old building."

I needed something to focus on besides the heat and my racing heart. "I know you saw the picture of Moira at the Lacys'," I said to Shelby, "but how did you know her parents ignore her?"

Shelby stopped banging on the pipes and stood up. "It was thanks to you, actually. You got me thinking about why Moira would do this. Would it be because she didn't have any friends? I couldn't imagine anybody being that desperate for approval from her peers."

(Remember what I said about Shelby not being the best judge of what's normal? Yeah. I mean, who doesn't want friends? I suppose I really should ask, who *besides Shelby Holmes* doesn't want friends?)

"That led me to thinking about her family. This was before the Lacy connection. When I went online, and you know that I loathe depending on technology, I saw a headline about her father. He's president of a huge international investment company down on Wall Street. A type of job that must be demanding. He probably doesn't spend a lot of time at home." Shelby's voice sounded distant. She went over to a glass meter and banged on it for a few seconds.

"Granted, I already knew she came from money, but there had to be a reason she would go through all this trouble and I wondered if there was a connection. Why would someone do that? Why would they blackmail a teacher simply to get to me? Clearly, it had to be a desperate cry for attention."

"That or she's evil." I didn't even realize I said that out loud until Shelby pointed the flashlight in my direction.

"Probably a little bit of both," Shelby said in the darkness. "But imagine being in a house where you're genuinely ignored, and then your parents go on and on about the talents of some girl from your past. It would be extremely irritating. At least I assume it would be for someone like Moira. Personally, I wouldn't care if my parents praised someone else, nor if they thought someone was smarter than me, even if that was a pretty impossible feat."

"I guess . . ." It was really hard to breathe. My entire body was shaking now. I'll admit that I was scared. We were trapped in some room, I was crashing, and I had no idea how we were going to get out of this mess.

"I think you should sit down," Shelby suggested, shining her light on me once again.

I didn't protest and collapsed on the floor.

"There's a vent up there." Shelby pointed the flashlight to a corner of the room, where there was a small vent near the ceiling. "Maybe I could climb the pipes . . ." Shelby yelped

as she touched one of the pipes. "Never mind, they're entirely too hot. Instead, I'll focus on making more noise to see if I can stir anybody to come investigate. You rest."

Shelby started banging loudly on one of the pipes again. The noise matched the throbbing in my head. There was no way that my blood sugar was in a good condition right now. If I was traveling for the day, I'd have insulin and a glucagon rescue kit with me, but I was supposed to be home hours ago. I thought I'd be playing basketball by now. Actually, by this point, I would've played ball and eaten. And had something to drink. And then eaten some more.

My mouth felt dry.

Shelby stopped banging on the pipes and turned her attention to the boiler. She started pulling levers and doing her best to break something. Anything that would lead somebody to realize we were down here. Maintenance would make routine checks, right?

Oh please, let me be right.

"I'm really sorry, Watson." Shelby's voice seemed to come from another room. "I should've made sure that you had something to eat or drink. I was too consumed by this case and Moira's motives. I promise that I will get you out of here and get you the biggest bottle of juice, and whatever you want to eat."

Shelby's voice had a strange tone to it. It took me a second to realize that it was laced with worry. Which meant she didn't know how we were going to get out of there. And I was worse off than I thought.

Because if Shelby was that worried, I was really in trouble.

"I'll be all right," I said, every word an effort. "I think I might lie down for a bit." I leaned over and curled up on the hard concrete floor. The floor itself wasn't as warm as the air, but it didn't make me feel any better.

"You take it easy, Watson. I'm going to get us out of here." The banging on the pipes intensified. Then I heard something break. "I'm going to rip the needle off one of the valves; that should hopefully do it."

Shelby kept talking, probably an attempt to keep me awake. It was a battle I was losing. I didn't feel right. Why was I now feeling cold, when it had been so warm? Maybe Shelby found a fan? I was shivering. I wished I had a blanket to wrap around me. I reached up and touched my face, which was covered in sweat.

That was weird. Why was I sweating if I was so cold?

This had never happened before.

I was in trouble.

"Watson?" I heard Shelby call out my name, but it was like she was underwater. Or maybe I was the one underwater. I sensed that her hands were on my face, taking my temperature, but I couldn't really feel it. It was like I knew she was there, but I was somewhere else.

"Watson!" There was a light tapping on my cheek, but I couldn't keep my eyes open anymore. It took too much effort. All I wanted to do was drift away.

"WATSON!"

And that was the last thing I remembered.

# ⚘ CHAPTER ⚘
# 24

"JOHN." I HEARD A FAMILIAR VOICE IN THE DISTANCE AND felt a hand rubbing my cheek.

Slowly, I opened my eyes, blinking back the daylight.

"Mom?" I mumbled.

Mom was standing over me, her cheeks stained with tears. "Oh, honey, you're going to be okay." While it seemed like she was trying to assure me, I think she was saying it more to herself. "You're going to be just fine."

"What happened?" It was hard to form words. I felt groggy.

"Your blood sugar was so low, you had diabetic hypoglycemia."

"Oh . . . ," I replied. I didn't have the energy to say or ask anything else.

"What do you remember?" Mom asked.

My mind was a bit foggy, but then I slowly remembered that Shelby and I had been locked in a boiler room.

"Shelby!" I exclaimed as I sat up. It was then that I realized that I was on a gurney, near an ambulance, and had an IV in my arm. I had to lie back down because I was too dizzy . . . and confused. "Where's Shelby?"

"She's over there." Mom looked over her right shoulder.

A paramedic came by and checked my vitals. It took me a few moments to take in the scene. We were outside Moira's apartment building. There was another ambulance next to mine. Shelby was sitting up on a gurney. Her arms were wrapped in gauze and her right arm was in a sling. "What happened to Shelby?" I asked. Even saying those few words took too much energy.

"She . . ." Mom's eyes welled up again. "I think she saved your life."

She *WHAT*? But how? She didn't have cell reception. The pipes were too hot to climb . . . Had the broken needle on the boiler done it? I looked over again at the gauze on Shelby's arms.

"How did we get out?" I asked Mom. It had seemed hopeless, although deep down I knew Shelby would find a way.

Shelby glanced at me. I tried to raise my hand to her to signal that I was going to be okay, but she quickly looked down at the ground.

"Shelby wrapped herself in clothes, climbed the pipes, and then set off some sort of smoke bomb near the vent, which is how maintenance realized someone was locked in the room. Once they got you out, Shelby called an ambulance and then called me. She suffered some pretty bad burns climbing the pipes."

I forgot that we had that second smoke bomb in her bag. "Why is her arm in a sling?"

"She fell the first time she climbed the pipes and dislocated her shoulder."

I can't believe Shelby did all of that for me. I wanted to talk to her and find out everything.

"I don't even want to think about what would've happened if Shelby hadn't been there," Mom said, tears spilling down her cheeks again.

I didn't want to think about that, either.

I'd had low blood sugar before, but it never got so bad that I'd lost consciousness. I'm just lucky it wasn't so bad that I started having seizures or . . .

Whoa. Shelby really did save my life.

Mom took a few moments to compose herself. "I'm so grateful to Shelby and relieved that you're going to be okay, John, but . . ." She placed her head in her hands. "What were you even doing in there? You were supposed to be at the museum."

I can't believe I'd done this to Mom. Not only was she upset at what had happened to me, I had lied to her. A lot.

This proved Mom was right: I shouldn't get involved in other people's messes. But how could I explain the rush that working with Shelby gave me? That I learned more in the past few weeks with Shelby than I'd ever learned from anybody.

"I'm sorry, Mom." I squeezed her hand.

"We need to have a long talk. But that can wait. The most important thing right now is for you to get better."

"Okay." I knew I was in trouble, but after everything that happened, maybe it would be better if I were grounded. At least at home, Moira Hardy couldn't get to me. At least I hoped she couldn't.

Even though I had a pounding headache, I sat myself up (successfully this time). I looked over at Shelby again and saw that she was talking to someone. That person was writing everything down in a notebook.

Wait a minute. It couldn't have been . . . No! It was!

Detective Lestrade!

That was when I realized there were other police officers around.

We were in so much trouble.

It was just our luck that out of all the police detectives that could've been called in for this case, we got Detective Lestrade. She would definitely take Moira's side on this, since she and Shelby couldn't stand each other.

Lestrade must've sensed me staring because she looked up and smiled at me. This had to be a figment of my imagination. While I'd never done anything to warrant Lestrade's wrath, I was an accomplice of Shelby's and therefore guilty by association.

Lestrade and Shelby exchanged a few more words, then Lestrade made her way over to me and Mom.

(And here I didn't think this day could get any worse.)

"What are we going to do, Detective?" Mom asked. "I want the girl who trapped my son to be held accountable for what she did. I want her locked up!"

Lestrade gave my mom a tight smile before turning her attention to me. "How are you feeling, John?"

"I'm feeling better." And confused. And a little worried about what was going to happen to us.

Lestrade tucked her pen behind her ear, her hair pulled up in a messy bun. "That's good." She looked at Mom, who had her arms

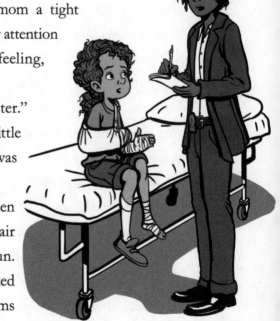

crossed and was clearly not going to be satisfied until she saw Moira hauled off in handcuffs. Come to think of it, I'd like to see that, too. "I'm afraid it's not so simple, Dr. Watson. Shelby and John were trespassing in this building. The family has said they won't press charges for"—Lestrade looked down at her notebook—"harassment and unlawful entry, as long as you leave. Their daughter, Moira, was almost too hysterical to get a statement from. Her tears were a bit much if you ask me. However, she swears she didn't see them or know they were in the boiler room."

"That's not true!" I protested. "She's the one who locked us in there!"

"I'm afraid there's not much we can do," Lestrade replied. "The only real evidence we have is that you and Shelby were in the building without permission. The doorman can testify that you entered unlawfully. And well . . ." Lestrade looked over at the other officers. "It's Park Avenue. It's the Upper East Side. I'm afraid these officers are going to take the word of a wealthy resident over yours."

Moira was going to get away with it.

She did it. She bested us.

"This is ridiculous!" Mom threw her hands up.

"I've done all I can by talking to the officers on the case," Lestrade said, and I believed her. She seemed as frustrated as Mom at how unfair it all was.

That had to mean that Lestrade believed us. That must've been why Shelby was talking to her.

But wait. If Lestrade wasn't working the case, what was she doing here?

"This isn't your case?" I asked.

"No. Shelby called and said she needed my help."

I had to lie down again. I was clearly hallucinating, because there was no way Shelby would ever ask Lestrade for help. Ever.

# CHAPTER
# 25

I DIDN'T KNOW WHAT WAS WORSE: UNDERSTANDING THAT I could've really been hurt or waiting for my punishment.

Even though I was feeling a lot better the next day, Mom made me stay home from school. She didn't go to work, and I spent all day taking naps, reading, and writing in my journal. And talking to Dad.

"You're looking better," Dad said during our third video chat since I got home. "I'm so sorry I wasn't there for you, John. But I talked to my boss, and I'm going to come visit in a few weeks. How does that sound?"

"Really?" I smiled. I was supposed to go to Kentucky to spend Thanksgiving with Dad, but this way I'd get to see him even sooner. And I'd get to show him around the neighborhood. He'd meet my friends. I could tell him all about Shelby.

Shelby.

I still hadn't had a chance to talk to her. I wanted to thank her for what she did. I also wanted to know what we were going to do now. Shelby didn't seem like the type of person to ever admit defeat, although she'd probably never lost before. I was also desperate to find out why she asked Detective Lestrade for help.

Out of everything that had happened, that was the thing that confused me the most.

"You make a list of the things you want to do while I'm there. Maybe we could catch a Knicks game?" Dad suggested.

"Yeah, that would be cool!" I glanced over at Mom, who was pretending to read a book, but I could tell she was listening in. "And I want you to meet my friends."

"Can't wait. I have a few words for that Shelby girl," Dad said with a laugh.

Mom grimaced at the mention of Shelby's name. I couldn't blame Shelby for not stopping by. While Mom was grateful to her for saving me, she also blamed Shelby for what had happened. "I knew she was nothing but trouble," Mom had said last night after I told her everything about Mr. Crosby, Ms. Semple, the watch, and Moira. "You never would've been in that mess if you were with your other friends instead of snooping around on some *case*."

I couldn't argue with her. But still, it wasn't fair. I *wanted* to go with Shelby. She even tried to get me to leave, but *I* was the one who insisted on staying.

"Shelby's something else, but she saved me, Dad," I said loudly enough to make sure Mom heard.

"I know, buddy." Dad gave me a smile as he reached out to touch the screen. I'd never wanted Dad to be here more than I did now. "My break is over and duty calls. Chat tonight?"

"Sounds great."

We hung up and I went over to the couch, grabbed my journal, and wrote down everything that I could remember from yesterday. Mom had filled me in on what Shelby and Detective Lestrade had told her about what happened after I blacked out. Although there were still a few things I didn't know.

There was a knock on our door a little after four. Mom got up from her computer to answer it. I almost didn't want to look as I had a feeling Mom wasn't going to be pleased to see Shelby.

But instead, she turned around and gave me a smile. "Hello, guys!" She opened the door wide, and there were Jason, Carlos, John Wu, and Bryant. "Come on in! Can I get you anything?" she asked.

"No thanks. We're just here to see how the hero's doing!"

Jason exclaimed with his chest puffed out, like he was swelling with pride.

*Hero?* Was he being sarcastic? I would've thought Carlos would be the one to give me grief.

"Wonderful," Mom said with a laugh. "Just try not to work him up too much. He's still not one hundred percent."

I cleared my throat, letting them all know that I could hear them. I was only about twenty feet away and tired, not deaf.

"Hey, Watson!" Carlos came over and lifted his hand for a high five. "What's going on with the Academy's newest legend?"

Yep. I knew Carlos wouldn't be able to resist a sarcastic dig.

John Wu sat down next to me on the couch. "You have to let me interview you next time I'm assigned a hero role. To actually get in the head of someone who is brave."

Ah. *Et tu, John?* (Did I use that right?)

"We thought it was cool playing on the same court as legends. Meanwhile you were becoming one," Jason chimed in.

"Ha-ha," I said drily.

"Come on, man! Stop being so modest. This is too awesome," Jason continued. "Your online journal is going to get so many hits when you write about this."

"Online journal?" Mom asked from the corner.

Busted.

(I'd conveniently left my journal out of our conversation last night.)

"Yeah, although it's more like *The Great John Watson*!" Carlos teased. We all knew there wasn't anything great about what I did. Which was nothing.

Bryant nodded. "Yeah. Or *The Indestructible John Watson*! Incredible job, man. Although it would've been cool if you'd let us in on your plans."

"Yeah . . ." I couldn't think of what to say. How did they know what happened yesterday? It wasn't like Shelby was one to talk to people at school.

"The dude who single-handedly saved Shelby Holmes is speechless!" John Wu nudged me.

Wait, what? They thought *I* saved Shelby? They really thought that I was the one who was a legend? They had it all wrong! Hero? Great? Indestructible? Those words should be used to describe Shelby, not me.

"Yeah, I guess Shelby isn't so smart after all," Bryant stated with a satisfied smile.

I looked over at Mom, who appeared as confused as I felt. And not only about my online journal.

"What?" I asked, trying to figure out what they were talking about. "What did you hear about yesterday?"

Carlos plopped down on the floor and started looking at my video games (all four of them). "That you guys were stuck in some basement because of a case and then, like, you had to scale a wall to get out. That's so rad. I mean we just play heroes in games, but you're one for real."

*What?!* Okay, so I wasn't completely with-it yesterday, but I knew everything they said was a lie. Where on earth would they have heard that?

"How did you . . ."

"*Everybody* at school is talking about it nonstop," Bryant filled me in. "I mean, we knew something was up when Shelby showed up at school with her arms messed up, and then it was over the entire school by lunch."

The only other person at school beside Shelby who knew everything that happened was Mr. Crosby. No way was he broadcasting this fake story.

So if I took a page out of Shelby's book and made deductions . . . the most reasonable explanation would be that Shelby was the one spreading that rumor around school. There was no other scenario that made sense. It had to have been her.

But why would Shelby lie?

# ↶ CHAPTER ↷
# 26

IF I WAS CONFUSED WHEN I WOKE UP OUTSIDE MOIRA'S apartment building, then I don't know what to call how I felt once the guys left.

They kept telling me about how I had saved the day, and asking me questions I couldn't answer. I didn't know what to say so I faked a headache, and Mom made them leave. While it was nice to be thought of as a hero, I should've said something to correct them. I needed to be done with lying. I just wasn't sure where to begin.

It seemed that I wasn't the only one.

"I don't even know how to make this up to you," Mr. Crosby said on the phone later that evening. It was his second call that day. He talked to Mom in the morning when I was napping. "I never should've involved you and Shelby."

But that was precisely what Moira wanted to happen. We'd all been played.

"I don't think Shelby really gave you a choice," I said,

trying to make light of everything. Besides, none of this was Mr. Crosby's fault.

He sighed. "I still can't believe what Shelby told me. That anybody, especially a former student of mine, would be capable of doing such a thing. Please know that I would never, and I mean never, want you to be put in any danger."

"All part of the job," I reassured him, even though of course *I* never thought I was going to put my life in danger, either. All for a watch. It stung that we went through all of that and were still empty-handed.

"Again, I'm so sorry, John. Please let me know if there's anything I can do."

"Thanks. I guess I'll see you tomorrow."

After a few more apologies from Mr. Crosby, we hung up. As I went to finish the homework that Jason had brought for me, I heard a light rapping on the front door. I walked over to my bedroom door and stopped when I heard voices.

"Hi, Shelby. Are you here to see John?" I heard Mom ask.

"On the contrary, I've come to speak with you, Dr. Watson."

I heard the door close and footsteps in the living room. I tiptoed into the hallway so I could hear better.

"I'm very sorry for the situation John was placed in

yesterday. He's doing better?" Shelby's voice was different. It wasn't filled with its usual vibrato. She was nervous, self-conscious, and unsure of herself.

"Yes, he is. While I know that I should be grateful to you, and I am——"

Shelby interrupted her. "I am entirely to blame for yesterday. I kept John out longer than originally planned. I didn't think about his diabetes until it was too late. That's why I wanted to talk to you. I've ensured that my backpack is now properly stocked with water, juice, and snacks for him, but I was hoping you could give me a glucagon rescue kit for emergency purposes."

There was a pause. "That would probably be a good idea, but Shelby, John won't be helping you on any more of your cases. He lied to me and said he wasn't doing any detective work. He had my permission to go to the dog show last month, and that was it. He never told me he was still working with you. He's never defied me before, and since we've moved here, well . . . I don't like that he's started to deceive me. I can't help but think this is your doing."

I almost ran into the living room to let Mom know that Shelby never forced me into anything. Okay, so I wasn't thrilled about having to set off that smoke bomb, but I could've said no. I could've walked away. But I didn't.

"Well, Dr. Watson, it seems that you weren't the only one

being lied to, as I wasn't aware that John hadn't told you about our cases."

That was the truth. How many secrets was I keeping? Maybe Mom was right. I never lied before we moved here.

Shelby continued. "My parents were hesitant when I first began taking cases, but people need my help. I provide a very useful service."

"One that you can continue, but not with my son," Mom replied with a tone that said *don't challenge me.*

Unfortunately (or maybe fortunately?), Shelby wasn't so easily persuaded. "I completely understand, but I think you need to know that your son is very bright. And that's about as high a commendation as somebody can get from me."

I couldn't believe it. It *was* the biggest compliment Shelby could give someone. I always figured Shelby needed me for the nongenius tasks: relating to people, knowing about normal things like sports, how friends act, etc. But would she really trust somebody to work with her who she didn't think was smart? I never thought of that before.

"I'd be lost without Watson, truly." Shelby's voice was soft. "And, in a way, he's making me a better person. Your son cares about people. People respond to him, and that's something that can't be taught in a book. You should be proud of him."

"I am," Mom stated. "But not about the lying."

"Yes, he lied to you, but he knew how much help I needed. I, of course, refused to believe that I would ever need help. But your son was the first person who wasn't threatened by my skills. He's the only person to ever be a friend to me, a *real* friend. Most of the time when people are nice to me it's because they want something. Not John. I've never had that before. I've never had a true friend before."

There was a pause, and I thought I heard a sniffle. I couldn't tell who it was from: Mom? Shelby?

It couldn't be Shelby. She didn't cry.

She also had never opened up to someone like she was doing right now.

"I hate that his trust in me got us into yesterday's predicament, but I once promised him that I would never let anything happen to him. And I meant it. We had a setback, but there was no way I was going to sit and watch him slip away."

"Shelby," Mom started.

"No, please listen. I don't make many mistakes, Dr. Watson, but on that very rare occurrence when I do, I learn from them. Which is why I'm here now asking you to help me manage his diabetes if we're ever in a difficult quandary again."

Mom was silent, while my head was spinning. Shelby could've written me off. She could've gone back to working cases alone, but she wanted me there. She wasn't one for sentimental mush, but everything she had said meant the world to me.

Mom finally spoke. "I'll give you a few things, but I still don't want him working on cases, Shelby. I appreciate everything you've said, but my answer is still no."

I leaned against the wall, feeling the worst I'd felt all week (which was saying a lot).

"Okay," Shelby relented, and I was disappointed she didn't fight harder. "However, I think you're underestimating your son."

I heard Mom sigh. I felt like I had to do something. Maybe it was time to finally be a hero (or at least not a coward who was hiding).

"Hey!" I called out as I walked into the living room. "I didn't know you were here."

"Yes," Shelby said. Her demeanor changed from concerned to bored. "Just wanted to make sure you were all right."

"Yeah, thanks, Shelby, for what you did." It was my first time seeing her up close. Both arms were completely bandaged, as was one ankle, and her right arm was in a sling. She must've really hurt herself trying to save me. "Are *you* okay?"

She waved me away with her good arm. "I'm fine."

She didn't look fine. She looked way worse than I did. My skin was still a little ashen, but besides that, I was the same old John Watson.

"I can't believe—"

"You seem to forget that I was also trapped, Watson. Let's not make this all about you."

The hard-edged Shelby exterior had returned. I was glad I overheard her talking to Mom, to know that she truly did appreciate me. And despite what she said, I knew she went through all that pain because of me.

"Well, I figure I at least owe you some chocolate," I offered. She wasn't going to accept my gratitude, but she was never one to turn down sugar. "Maybe we could hit up Levain after school tomorrow?"

The corner of her lips twitched. "Yes, well, I did put myself in a rather precarious position, so that would be a suitable form of appreciation."

Mom walked away shaking her head. She could prevent me from working on Shelby's cases, but she couldn't stop me from being her friend. And I knew there had to be a way to get Mom to let me partner with Shelby again . . . even though I never had her permission in the first place.

"Are you going to school tomorrow?" Shelby asked. "I suppose you could probably milk another day or two if you wanted."

"Naw, I figure it's time to get back to school. Although I'm sure there are plenty of stories going around about what happened." I smiled at Shelby.

She could play tough and nonplussed all she wanted, but I knew the truth: Shelby Holmes really cared about me.

# CHAPTER
# 27

SITTING ON THE FRONT STEPS OUTSIDE OUR BROWNSTONE had become a familiar routine for me. When I first moved to 221 Baker Street, I sat there out of boredom, but I also did it because I was hoping to hang out with Shelby.

So there I was the next morning, sitting on the steps waiting to walk to school with her. I was also itching to get her alone so I could finally get the answers to all my questions.

Shelby didn't even pause when she exited the building. "Feeling better?"

"Yeah, thanks." I couldn't believe Shelby was acting like it was any other day. Then I notice something: Shelby's worn purple backpack had been replaced with a newer one. "You got a new backpack?"

"Yes!" Shelby exclaimed, a little more enthusiastically than I was expecting. "I see that you're finally observing. Well done, Watson!"

I think a huge, bright, new purple backpack would be hard for anyone to miss. "What happened to your old one?" She had carried that thing with her everywhere. It held her entire life and all her detective tools.

"It broke on Monday."

It broke when we were out? I didn't remember—

*Oh.*

"How did it break?" I wanted to hear what happened directly from Shelby.

"Well, I wrongly assumed that if I wrapped the backpack straps around the pipe I could use them to hold on to the pipe, while I used my feet to shimmy up. It worked for a while. I was almost to the top when the straps broke." She looked down at her right arm in the sling.

"That's when you dislocated your shoulder?"

"Correct. I wasn't prepared to fall, which was entirely my fault, and I landed wrong."

"That must've hurt."

Shelby shrugged it off. "It wasn't pleasant. It was worse when I popped it back into place. But time was of the essence, so there was no time for a pity party. I wrapped my arms up using my Basia costume and climbed the pipe the old-fashioned way."

I stopped walking.

"Shelby . . ." I couldn't find the right words. How do you

thank somebody for putting herself through so much to save you?

"We're going to be late, Watson," Shelby called over her shoulder as she kept walking.

I jogged to catch up to her. There was still so much I needed to know. "So what are we going to do? Did Moira return the watch to Mr. Crosby like she said she would? And why were you talking to Lestrade?" I began firing questions.

"*We* aren't going to do anything. You never told me that your mom didn't know you were working with me," Shelby snapped. Honestly, I think the fact she hadn't deduced that I was lying to my mom upset her more than anything.

I didn't have a response. I should've told Mom. Maybe I should've let Shelby know that I hadn't told Mom. I should've done a *bunch* of things differently, but none of that changed the situation we were in now. "But I want to help you. I'll talk to—"

"Listen, Watson," Shelby cut me off. "I would love your help, and while I'm no stranger to being creative when it comes to informing my parents of my activities, I can't put you in danger like that again. Your mom has already lost—" Shelby stopped herself.

"My mom has lost what?" I asked, worry in my voice. Shelby could always tell things about people by merely looking at them. She saw something in my mom, and I wanted to know what it was. "You have to tell me, Shelby!"

She hesitated for a minute. "It's been difficult on your mom to raise you by herself these last few months. I know you miss your father, but you need to realize that she misses him as well. And if anything happened to you, she'd truly be alone."

For the second time that week, I felt out of breath. But this was different. It was like the wind had been knocked out of me. Shelby knew more about my mom than I did.

"I'll handle Mr. Crosby. Don't worry about it," Shelby assured me.

"But, but I . . . ," I stuttered. As much as I wanted to help her, I couldn't without Mom's permission. It wasn't fair to keep lying to Mom when she'd done so much for me. And I knew I was *never* getting Mom's permission.

We stayed silent until we turned the corner of the school. A few of our fellow students stopped what they were doing when they saw us and started whispering. Some even pointed.

"Why did you tell people that I saved you?" I asked Shelby.

She had to have known I'd hear the rumors.

"I figured it would be a blow to your delicate male ego to have been saved by a girl."

That didn't make sense. I didn't care about something

like that. And Shelby wasn't one to shrug off credit, or not show how smart she was. "Shelby, come on. Why would you do that? You know I'm going to write about all of this eventually."

"You care about the opinions of your peers more than I do."

"But I'm going to tell everybody the truth."

Yeah, I was going to make things right with the *truth*. First I'd let people know it was Shelby who saved me. Second, I'd find a way to make everything up to my mom.

"Shelby, what's the *real* reason?"

Shelby turned to me before we entered the front doors of the school. People were definitely looking at us.

"It's not a big deal," Shelby said, even though it *was* a big deal. Then in a quiet voice she added, "Plus, you *have* saved me. In your own way."

# CHAPTER
# 28

EVERYBODY WAS LOOKING AT ME. PEOPLE STARED AS I walked to my locker. I should've walked with my head held high, since everybody assumed that I was some big hero. What a joke that was.

"Watson!" Tamra Lacy called out to me as I grabbed my books. "How are you? Oh my goodness, I can't get over what you did." She gave me a wide smile as her friends stood behind her giggling.

"Er, thanks, but it was Shelby," I replied. "She was the hero, not me."

"Oh, that makes sense."

Yep, because Tamra had seen Shelby in action. She knew better.

I hadn't really talked to Tamra since she basically ignored me on the first day of school. I was about to ask how Zane was, if he was still grounded for dognapping Daisy, but there was something else I wanted to know. "Hey, you know Moira Hardy, right?"

"Yeah, our dads are friends. How do *you* know Moira?"

"I ran into Moira the other day." I decided to remain fuzzy on the details. Shelby was always coy about her cases until they were solved, and I didn't know how much to share.

Tamra laughed. "Yeah, well, I'm sure you had a great time," she said sarcastically. "She makes Zareen look like an angel." Zareen was Tamra's older sister, and to say that they fought was like saying Shelby knew a few things.

"How so?" I asked.

"Anytime her parents give even the smallest compliment to somebody else she goes off. My mom says it's because she's an only child."

Um, I was an only child and would never behave that way. In fact, I didn't know one sane person who would act like that, siblings or not.

"Oh!" Tamra flipped her hair. "Speaking of which. Her dad was superimpressed by the way you and Shelby got to the bottom of figuring out who took Daisy. So maybe you should watch your back, Watson!"

She laughed lightly, then continued down the hall to her first class. If only Shelby and I had that information two days ago. So much would be different.

Too little, much too late.

• • •

All morning at school I got high fives and nods of respect. A few girls even told me how brave I was. Normally I'd love the attention ... if it weren't all a lie. I kept replying, "Thanks, but it was all Shelby." Most people would respond with a laugh and go on their way. We really needed to get to the bottom of this case so I could report on the entire truth of what happened.

When the bell rang at the end of science class, Shelby sprinted out of the room while Mr. Crosby asked me to stay for a second.

"How are you feeling?" Mr. Crosby asked for the third time so far today. (He was waiting for me at my locker before school, then when I walked into class, and now.) "You look better!"

He hardly glanced at me during class. When he did, he looked guilty.

"I'm doing better, thanks." I noticed his bare wrist. "So ... have you heard from Moira yet about your watch?"

"No," Mr. Crosby replied. "But it's nothing you need to worry about. It's only a watch. It wasn't worth what you went through. Again, I'm so sorry."

"It's okay." Even though it wasn't.

We failed Mr. Crosby. What was worse was that Moira got away with everything with zero consequences.

"I should get to my next class," I said.

"Of course, of course." Mr. Crosby stood up and walked me to the hallway. "Again, please let me know if there's anything I can do. And I'm so sorry. For everything."

I gave him a smile as I turned to walk down the hallway. But Mr. Crosby called after me, "You're very brave, John."

That wasn't true. Mr. Crosby knew the real story about what happened on Monday.

I wasn't brave. I was a fraud.

But that was going to change. I had to finally do the right thing. The scary thing.

I had to tell Mom everything.

# CHAPTER 29

"Do you have a second?" I asked Mom after dinner while we were cleaning up. We had our routine. Mom washed while I dried and put the dishes away.

"I always have time for you. Are you feeling all right?" Mom asked, her forehead creasing.

"Yes, it's just . . . I need you to know a few things. I want you to know the truth about working with Shelby. All of it."

Mom took the frying pan from me and set it on the counter. She put her arm around my shoulder as I sat down at the table.

"When I first came here, I was really lost," I admitted. "I was overwhelmed. I know I pretended to be okay with everything, but I didn't know what to think. Everything had changed so quickly." Mom nodded in agreement. "Shelby took care of me. Helping with her cases has been amazing. I'm learning a lot and doing something different. I'm doing something that matters."

I opened up Mom's laptop and pulled up my online journal. "I want you to know about the cases we've done together. It's all here. I've been writing about them for class. I know I should've told you about my journal, but I was worried if you knew about the cases that you wouldn't let me keep working with Shelby. And Mom, I just . . . *needed* to. But now you can read this and see everything that she can do, and how I'm helping her. Mom, I'm a part of something really special."

Mom started scrolling down my posts. "John, I know Shelby is really smart, but you got very sick because you were working with her. You've lied to me about where you've been, what you were doing, who you're—" Mom stopped, then looked at me. "I just realized something: Basia wasn't Mrs. Hudson's niece."

"No. It was Shelby."

Mom looked impressed for a second before shaking it off.

"I know you're worried," I said. "Believe me, I was worried in the boiler room, too, but it wasn't Shelby's fault. *I* was the one who knew my blood sugar was low. *I* was the one who followed Shelby when she told me to leave. If I was with anybody else when I was locked in that boiler room, well, I think we both know what would've happened."

Tears started welling in Mom's eyes.

"I trust Shelby," I said. "In fact, I trust her more than ever now." And come to think of it, maybe more than I trust anybody outside of Mom. Shelby had never lied to me (she'd lied *for* me). She had my back, and put herself in danger to help me. "But I need *you* to trust *me*," I finished.

Mom was wringing her hands. I knew she just didn't want anything to happen to me. After all, she was my mom.

My mom who had lost a big part of her life already. I kept thinking about what Shelby said. That I was all Mom had, and I had put myself in harm's way.

So I decided to take the biggest risk, and talk about the thing we'd both been avoiding. The thing we both lost.

"I'm sad about Dad," I said, and Mom snapped her head up to look at me. "I miss him. And I know it's been hard on you, too. I'm sorry. But I want you to know that I'm not going anywhere."

Mom began to rub my back, and I did my best to shake off the tears that were stinging behind my eyes. I had to be strong for her. "But I know that now it's just you and me. And that means I need to step up. No more lies, okay?"

Tears were flowing down Mom's cheeks. "I'm so proud of the man you're turning into," she said.

Maybe it was spending so much time with Shelby, but I was feeling pretty proud of myself, too.

"Do you trust me?" I pressed Mom.

She wiped away her tears and stood up to face me. Vulnerable Mom was gone, and Tough Mom had returned. "I do trust you, John. And you're not the only one who is going to make some changes. First, while I still think you're too young, I know we're in a different time from when I was a kid, so you'll be getting your own cell phone."

*Whoa.* I didn't see that coming.

"So we can be in constant contact. I need to know where you are at all times. No more lies," she repeated my promise.

I couldn't believe I was finally getting a phone. It made me feel super grown-up (and yeah, a little cool to finally have one).

"So . . ." Mom closed her eyes. "You can still work with Shelby, BUT!" She held out her finger as I was about to jump up from the chair. "From here on out, you are to tell me about your cases, who you're working for, and what you're doing to solve the case. Deal?"

"Of course!"

I couldn't believe it. I got to continue working with Shelby *and* get a cell phone. Wow, things were really looking up for John Watson.

# CHAPTER 30

I PRACTICALLY SKIPPED UP THE FLIGHT OF STAIRS TO Shelby's after talking with Mom. I couldn't wait to tell Shelby that I could still work with her. Maybe she already had a new case for us.

I knocked on the door and my mood diminished when Michael opened it. "Yes," he answered with his usual bored tone.

"Hi, Michael. Is Shelby here?" I asked.

"Is Earth 365 million miles away from Jupiter?" he asked.

I replied with a blank stare until he finally held open the door for me. (So I take it that was a yes?)

Classic music filled the apartment as Michael returned to an armchair to continue reading some ginormous book on philosophy. Had anybody in this house ever cracked opened a Harry Potter book?

I went upstairs, where the sound of the violin got louder

as I climbed. I'd never heard Shelby play. Classical music wasn't my thing, but I was pretty impressed by what I heard. She really was good.

I hadn't been on the second floor of the Holmeses' apartment yet. I was sort of curious to see Shelby's bedroom. There was no way it was going to be a normal room. There was a master bedroom off to the right, and two doors to the left that were closed. One door had a Do Not Enter by Credence of Shelby Holmes sign taped to it.

I reached out my fist to knock, but before I could do it, Shelby's voice came from behind the door. "Come on in, Watson."

How did—

You know what? Never mind. Why did I keep asking questions like that? Of *course* she somehow knew I was outside her bedroom. I think I should just refer to her abilities like a verb. *There she goes again, pulling a Shelby.*

I opened the door and took a sweep of her room. It was exactly how I hoped it would be: organized chaos. Along one wall were two bookshelves that were crammed with so many books, the shelves were drooping. On the other side of the room was a desk that was covered with stacks of paper, a few glass beakers, and what appeared to be a toolbox. Sir Arthur was asleep on top of her unmade bed, which was pushed next to the only window in the room. The room was

sparsely decorated: there was a poster of the periodic table, a quote that read, "When you have eliminated the impossible, whatever remains, *however improbable*, must be the truth," and random pieces of paper tacked to the wall. Shelby was seated with her violin near the door.

Shelby returned to playing her violin. She had to bend down so her hand with the bow, which was the arm with the sling, could reach the violin. Even in that weird position she was amazing.

"You're really good." I gestured at her violin.

She stopped playing. "I know. It drives your friend crazy."

Hmm. Maybe if Shelby showed a bit more humility, people like Moira wouldn't be out to get her.

"So I have good news!"

"Well, it is about time that you officially got your mother's permission to work with me."

How did she . . . ?

*There she goes, pulling another Shelby.*

"Yeah! So . . . any new cases yet? Anything you want me to study?" I couldn't believe I was *asking* Shelby for homework, but I wanted to start working on another case. One that we could actually solve.

"I have an arrangement with my parents that during the school year I only work on one case at a time."

"So you're working on one now?"

"I haven't closed my last case."

She couldn't have meant . . .

"But Moira said she was going to return Mr. Crosby's watch." Even though she hadn't contacted him yet.

"Yes, but she said that before you wound up in an ambulance. She has to be scared to even try to return the watch to him at school now. So I'm going to make it easier on her . . . and take it back."

She noticed the panicked look on my face. "Don't worry, Watson. This time it will be very simple. Moira would never expect me to revisit Miss Adler's. But that's exactly what I'm going to do."

"But how do you even know she has the watch with her?"

"She'll want to keep it close to her. As we witnessed, she put the watch in the inside pocket of her blazer, and I would presume it's more than likely that it has remained at her side since Monday. So I'm going to retrieve it when her blazer isn't on. While she's in gym. I'll have no problem getting into her locker. I'll take it back and then we can put this rather inconvenient case behind us."

"But how are you going to get into the school? Doesn't Ms. Semple know about Basia now?"

"Oh yes, Ms. Semple knows everything."

"Everything?"

"Everything." Then Shelby's confident demeanor faltered. "I had to do something that I'm not particularly proud of. It's something I had vowed to never, ever do. Ever."

What could be so bad that it would make Shelby ashamed?

Then it hit me.

"Lestrade?" I asked, and even the mention of her name made Shelby's face tense.

"Yes. While the 'detective'"—Shelby used air quotes—"and I don't always see eye to eye, she knew we were telling the truth on Monday. She didn't fall for Moira's naive act, like those police officers who were called in when we were discovered. So I asked for her help, which required her contacting Ms. Semple. Granted, I could've called her myself, but I felt when it came to matters of Moira Hardy, I should have someone with perceived authority get involved. Plus, I didn't want to have to listen to Ms. Semple drone on and on about how I should return to Miss Adler's."

"Please tell me you're going to get Moira kicked out of school." It was ridiculous that Moira was able to convince the police that we were the guilty ones.

"No. We need to think long term, Watson," Shelby stated. "While that was my initial reaction as well, Moira's the kind of person who needs to be busy or she'll find trouble. Believe me, I know a thing or two about that." I was thankful that Shelby used her smarts for good. "If we get her expelled, she'll no doubt spend her time trying to get even with us. No, what I require of Ms. Semple is simply access to the school on Friday."

"Does Ms. Semple believe us?"

"Yes. I gave Lestrade evidence that proved Moira hacked the school's e-mail system and accessed Ms. Semple's e-mail. Lestrade filled Semple in. As you can imagine, the headmistress wasn't very happy about one of her students behaving in such a way, but the girls in Moira's family have attended Miss Adler's for generations and donate a lot of money. Apparently, Ms. Semple couldn't expel Moira even if she wanted to. She will, however, be looking the other way on Friday."

Shelby's focus shifted down to her hands. There was something she wasn't telling me.

"That's the only reason you talked to Lestrade?"

She shook her head solemnly. "Lestrade will be accompanying us on Friday."

"Us?" I asked. Shelby didn't need me to help, but she wanted me to.

"You don't have to be there, Watson. But after what you've been through it only feels right. How does that sound?"

"Great!" Although I still didn't understand why Lestrade had to be there. Shelby could slip in and out of places quickly. She could pick whatever lock there was. "But why do we need—"

"You," Shelby replied in a small voice.

"What about me?" I asked, confused of what I had to do with any of this.

"Lestrade will be there to make sure nothing else happens to you. I underestimated Moira once, and that will be the last time. Moira's gym period lines up with our lunch, so Lestrade has agreed to escort us."

"Okay." It did make me feel a little better that we'd have backup. "Um, isn't breaking into a locker technically illegal?"

Shelby grimaced. "We are taking something back that was stolen. Lestrade offered to get a warrant to open Moira's locker to retrieve the watch herself, but I didn't want to deal with the lawyers that Moira's family would no doubt bring in. Plus, Lestrade understands that this is something we need to do on our own. So she'll be looking the other way as we finally get that watch. I promise, it'll be quick and easy."

So Moira wouldn't be expelled or have anything happen to her for what she did to me and Shelby, but we'd finally have Mr. Crosby's watch.

It wasn't the justice that I hoped for, but at least we'd have another satisfied customer.

"Quick and easy," Shelby repeated.

Yeah, I'd heard her say that before about getting the watch: quick and easy.

I could only hope that this time it would be true.

# CHAPTER
# 31

"YOU LOOK A LOT BETTER THAN WHEN I LAST SAW YOU," Lestrade commented as I walked to her unmarked cop car during lunch on Friday.

"Thanks," I replied, not used to her being so friendly to me.

"But I see that you're still hanging out with Shelby, despite my best efforts."

I remained silent. I did ignore her warning when we first met that I should stay away from Shelby. Was she mad?

Lestrade let out an uncharacteristic laugh. "I can't blame you. I think you'd be surprised to know that I was just like Shelby when I was younger. Always getting myself into other people's business. Although I wasn't as good a sleuth as she is."

WHAT? I stood there with my mouth open. I couldn't believe it. This week just kept getting more bizarre by the minute.

Shelby walked out of the building, accompanied by Mr. Crosby.

"Are you sure about this?" Mr. Crosby asked.

"Of course," Shelby replied confidently as she got into the backseat of Lestrade's car.

Mr. Crosby shook hands with Detective Lestrade. "You'll make sure they stay safe?"

"Of course," Lestrade replied in the same confident manner before she got into the driver's seat.

Maybe Shelby and Lestrade weren't so different after all.

I slid into the seat next to Shelby.

"Everybody good?" Detective Lestrade asked as she pulled out in front of the school. I saw her grin at the sight of Shelby in the backseat. I wouldn't be surprised if the detective had wished on occasion that she could haul Shelby away in her car. Probably never thought they'd be working together.

That made three of us.

"Eat your lunch, Watson," Shelby ordered me as she placed my lunch bag on my lap. I doubt I'd ever miss a meal or a snack again with Shelby around.

The car ride down to Miss Adler's was a lot quicker than taking the bus, especially since on a couple occasions Lestrade used her siren to blow through stoplights. (I think she was showing off for Shelby since we weren't in any rush.

We had permission from our parents and the school to be late for our next class, which happened to be science with Mr. Crosby.)

Lestrade pulled up to the side entrance of Miss Adler's School, where deliveries were usually made. A white woman with black hair pulled tightly into a bun, and the straightest posture I'd ever seen, was waiting for us.

Ms. Semple, I presume?

"Shelby!" Ms. Semple exclaimed. "I had absolutely no idea that was you on Monday. My goodness, you are an expert at disguise. I feel so silly for not recognizing one of the most brilliant students Miss Adler's ever had the pleasure to teach. I simply can't believe it!"

I wanted to pat her on the back and say, *I know, I* know.

"Yes, well, that is the point of a disguise, Ms. Semple," Shelby replied with a loud snort.

"And you must be John." Ms. Semple extended her hand to me. "I'm so sorry for everything you've been through. I hope this will bring a close to this unsettling business with Moira once and for all."

Me too.

"Shall we?" Ms. Semple asked as she opened the door.

"I'll be out here if you need anything," Lestrade said to us before we went inside.

The hallways of Miss Adler's were silent. The only sound

was the click of Ms. Semple's shoes as she took us to a door. "They've been in class for several minutes now. Nobody should be in the locker room, but you should proceed with caution. I don't mind getting maintenance to open her locker for you."

"I'd prefer to handle this myself," Shelby replied.

"Of course. I am sorry for all your trouble, Shelby. Unfortunately, with Moira, our hands are tied."

Ms. Semple's eyes darted to the end of the hallway, where I saw a large plaque outside a door that read The Hardy Auditorium.

Man, I knew that money could buy you lots of stuff, but I never realized how much trouble it could get you out of.

Shelby gave Ms. Semple a tight smile. "We never had this conversation, and you never saw us."

"You know, Shelby, we would just love to have you if you would ever reconsider—"

"Yes, I know. The answer is still no." Shelby turned on her heels, and she slowly opened the locker room door. She peered around the corner, then gave me the sign that it was safe to enter.

Then I went where no sixth grade boy (that I knew of) had gone before: the girls' locker room. I don't know what I expected, but it was like any other locker room: lockers lining the walls, benches in front, and a separate room for showers and bathroom stalls.

"Let's make this quick," Shelby whispered as we approached the lockers.

There were at least fifty small, pale green lockers along the wall. "How do we know which one is Moira's?"

"Easy," Shelby replied as she walked up to one with a huge lock on it. I scanned the others and noticed none of them had locks. It made sense that Moira wouldn't trust anybody with her stuff (which was smart since Shelby was currently looking through her tools to pick the lock).

"Stand guard to make sure nobody comes in," Shelby ordered me. "The door that leads to the gym is around the corner."

I tiptoed to the door. I heard the familiar sounds of sneakers squeaking on the hardwood floor, the occasional dribble of a ball, and muffled voices. (My own powers of deduction told me that they were playing basketball.) My attention shifted to a pair of sports goggles on the floor. I picked them up and realized they distorted the tile floor. So they were prescription sports goggles. Whoever dropped them must be having a hard time seeing.

*Oh no.* What if the girl came back to get her goggles? I heard the gym teacher call in different players. I listened at the door, and I thought I heard an older female voice say, "Well, go get them!" followed by the sound of footsteps approaching.

"Shelby!" I hissed and waved my arms, trying to get her attention, but she was hunched over working a long silver pick into the lock. I ran to her. "There's someone coming, Shelby! She dropped her goggles!"

"I'm sure it's nothing," Shelby dismissed me.

We were going to get caught. I just knew it.

I grabbed Shelby by the elbow of her left arm and dragged her away from the locker. "Watson!" she protested as I got us into one of the shower stalls. I pulled the curtain closed and put my hand over her mouth right as we heard the door to the locker room open.

Shelby's eyes were wide. I was right! If it weren't for me, we would've been caught! I saved the day!

ABOUT. TIME.

We heard someone walking around the locker room. "There they are!" the girl exclaimed before opening the door and venturing out to the gym again.

I waited a few beats before slowly pulling the curtain back to reveal we were once again alone.

*Phew.* That was close.

I looked at Shelby with a goofy grin on my face. She scowled before shrugging her shoulders nonchalantly. "Well done, Watson. Now, I'm not one for mollycoddling, so let's get on with it."

I had no idea what that meant, but I still needed to purse my lips together to hold in a laugh. It was clear Shelby was irritated that *I* saved us, but hey, it felt pretty great to be right.

"How much longer?" I asked in a low voice as Shelby approached the locker.

"It's already done," she replied as she yanked on the lock and it clicked open. Shelby quickly opened the locker, reached into the pocket of Moira's jacket, and pulled out Mr. Crosby's watch. She inspected it for a moment before placing it in her backpack.

Shelby gave me a nod that signaled that we were ready to go.

We did it! We were done!

I felt a wave of relief as I opened the door to the hallway, but then stopped cold.

There standing on the other side of the door, waiting for us, was Moira.

# CHAPTER 32

*YOU'VE GOT TO BE KIDDING ME.*

*No! No! No! NO!*

*HOW DID SHE KNOW WE WERE HERE?!*

"Hello, Shelby. Watson." Her lips were curled in a self-satisfied smirk. "Funny seeing you here."

"I'm surprised you can look us in the eye after what you did," Shelby said with a scowl on her face. Moira's confident demeanor faltered for a second as she glanced at Shelby's injuries. "Being intelligent requires one to foresee all possibilities. And for that, you failed."

"I bet you didn't see this coming?" Moira shot back at us.

That was true. Annoyingly so.

"In fact, I did," Shelby said with a bored look on her face.

"You know I can just steal that watch again."

"No, you can't. Mr. Crosby has been given a more secure location for his valuables, compliments of yours truly. If you try to take his watch again, you'll be caught, and your blubbering to the police won't work in my neighborhood. The police are smarter."

*Did Shelby just compliment Lestrade? Whoa.*

"Because they listen to me," Shelby continued.

*Okay, maybe not.*

Moira paused for a moment. She seemed unsure of what to do. (That made two of us.) "I'm going to scream so loudly, security is going to rush over. They'll detain you, and then I'll have a restraining order filed against the both of you."

Shelby laughed. Like, a real laugh. "I highly doubt that. *You* couldn't stay away from us even if you wanted to."

Moira took a deep breath while I braced myself for her scream. I was ready to run out of there, but Shelby remained stubbornly still.

Suddenly, Ms. Semple came racing down the hallway. "Miss Hardy, what are you doing out of class?"

Moira gave her a weird look. "I'm apprehending these two trespassers. It seems like some people don't know where they belong. I'd like to report them, Ms. Semple."

"What are you talking about?" Ms. Semple walked right up to Moira and folded her arms. Her gaze was fixated on Moira. She refused to acknowledge us.

"These two!" Moira pointed directly at us while stomping her foot.

Ms. Semple looked where Moira was pointing, her finger only a few inches away from Shelby's face. While there was no way she couldn't have seen us, it seemed like she was looking right through us.

"Miss Hardy," Ms. Semple said in a motherly voice, "I think we need to take you to the school nurse. You can't be feeling well."

"WHAT IS WRONG WITH YOU?" Moira began to throw a tantrum.

Shelby nudged me, and we started walking toward the exit. We could hear Moira protesting the entire way. At one point she even screamed, "Guards! They're getting away!"

I picked up my pace, while Shelby kept a casual stride. We reached the exit, and I finally felt the tension release from my shoulders once we stepped outside. Detective Lestrade was leaning on the front of her car. "Everything work out?"

"Of course," Shelby replied smugly as she got into the backseat of the car.

"Great, thanks." I gave Lestrade a smile since the detective was making an effort. Oh, and you know, she was the reason we were able to get into the school.

While Lestrade drove back to the Academy, I watched through the window with relief as Miss Adler's got farther away.

Shelby reached into her new backpack and handed me a bag of almonds. "Better have a snack."

Instead of arguing that I'd had lunch on the ride over, I ate the almonds.

"Here's some water." Shelby unzipped a cooler compartment inside her bag and gave me a chilled bottle of water. I noticed a couple vials of my insulin in the cooler.

Shelby's cell phone chirped. **"This isn't the last you've heard from me,"** she read out loud. "Oh, I'm counting on it," she responded as she typed a reply.

"How'd Moira get your number?"

"Told you she was clever," Shelby said with a wide smile on her face.

It was as if this was fun for Shelby. Yeah, she finally met someone who challenged her, but at what cost? What was going to happen next time we crossed Moira's path? I didn't even want to think about it.

"Don't worry, Watson. I won't underestimate her again. Plus, we won this round."

*Wait a second.*

"*Rounds?* I thought you didn't know anything about sports. That they couldn't take up precious real estate in your brain attic," I teased her.

"Merely checking to ensure you're paying attention," she retorted.

*Yeah, right.*

As we pulled up to the school, I realized that I should feel happy the case was over. And I was. But I was also wondering when we'd find another "worthy" case again, especially since I was getting better at deductive reasoning.

Lestrade let us out of the backseat.

Shelby gritted her teeth for a few moments before saying, "Thank you, Detective Lestrade, for all your help. We couldn't have done it without you."

Lestrade looked quite pleased with herself.

Maybe Shelby was finally listening to me about how to treat people. You give a person some respect and they'll respect you in return.

"Oh, and one more thing, Detective," Shelby said with a sweet smile.

Here we go. Just when I thought she learned something, Shelby was going to lob one of her patented zingers at Lestrade. One step forward, two steps back . . .

"Regarding the arson case in Morningside Heights that's been in the paper, it's the landlord who set fire to the restaurant. Check the lease and the hardware store down the block, and you'll have all the evidence you need."

Lestrade narrowed her eyes (while I reminded myself to go online and look up the fire), her face stubbornly set. Then her features softened. "We'll look into it. Thanks."

She held out her hand to Shelby, who took it, and the two shook.

Okay, scratch everything I had said before. *That* was the craziest thing I'd ever seen.

# ⌐ CHAPTER ⌐
# 33

A WEEK LATER, AND THINGS HAD RETURNED TO NORMAL.

Well, as normal as they can be when you're friends (and partners) with Shelby Holmes.

School was school. The homework kept growing, but so did the readership of my online journal. Mom was even reading about my adventures with Shelby. Her biggest critique: she didn't come across as funny in my writing as she was in real life. So please note, dear readers, that my mom is hilarious. She should be a comedian, she's that funny. (Okay, so sometimes knowing who your audience is can affect your writing.)

The rumors and whispers about me being a big hero also died down, since I did everything I could to let people know that it was really Shelby who was the hero.

Of course, the guys were never going to let me live it down.

"Shelby Holmes can't save you now!" Carlos taunted me as he scored a basket on me after school.

I gave him a cross look, something I had learned from Shelby, as I picked up the ball.

"Yeah, you— Oh." Carlos stopped cold in his tracks. "Um, hey, Shelby."

I turned around to see Shelby near the fence that bordered the court.

"Salutations, acquaintances of Watson's," Shelby replied with a tilt of her head.

I jogged over to Shelby. "Hey, what's up?" I asked, itching for our next case.

"Well, you seem to be engaged in a rather important matter. I wouldn't want to take you away," she remarked sarcastically.

"Ha-ha!" I replied with a roll of my eyes (it was nice to do that to her for a change). "I'll be right back."

I jogged over to the fellas. "Hey, guys, I gotta bounce." I threw Jason the ball.

"Is it a case?" Jason asked. "Y'all just keep getting bigger and bigger. What is it? No, wait! Don't tell me. I want to read all about it."

Carlos waved self-consciously at Shelby. "Do you think, like, she would ever need my help?"

Bryant groaned. "Seriously? I don't think she needs someone who can play video games for ten hours straight."

"And you just described my dream job."

"Okay, okay," I interrupted them. "I'll see you guys tomorrow!"

They all shouted *later* at me, while Jason and John Wu even said good-bye to Shelby. I was happy that my friends had started treating Shelby with a little more respect. And it wasn't just them. I hadn't heard the word *freak* whispered in Shelby's presence in days.

Shelby had an amused expression on her face.

"What?" I asked.

"Don't you find it exhausting?"

"What? Basketball?"

"No. Friendship."

"Come on, Shelby! It's not *that* bad, right?" I nudged her.

"It's tolerable," she sniffed. "On some days."

Well, that was about as good as I could expect.

I couldn't take it anymore. I had to know. "So what's going on?"

Then Shelby said my favorite sentence in the English language:

"We've got another case to solve."

# ACKNOWLEDGMENTS

As Shelby and Watson prove, it's better to be part of a team. I'm so fortunate to have the amazing crew at Bloomsbury in my corner, especially my publicist, Courtney Griffin. Thanks to Diane Aronson, Erica Barmash, Hali Baumstein, Beth Eller, Jessie Gang, Cristina Gilbert, Melissa Kavonic, Emily Klopfer, Jeanette Levy, Cindy Loh, Donna Mark, Lizzy Mason, Patricia McHugh, Brittany Mitchell, Emily Ritter, and Sarah Shumway. Cheers to the brilliant team in the UK: Vicky Leech, Nicholas Church, Anna de Lacey, Andrea Kearney, and Lizz Skelly.

Erwin Madrid's wonderful illustrations continue to bring Shelby and Watson to life, as well as a smile to my face (and sometimes a very ladylike snort).

Shelby would still be solely an idea in my head if it weren't for my agent Erin Malone's encouragement. The entire team at WME, especially Laura Bonner and Christina Raquel, have been a dream to work with (and the first people I'll call if I'm ever brought in to solve a crime).

I'm more like Watson when it comes to friends and family. I'm so fortunate to have so many author friends who have supported me for years. Huge vat of sugar to Jen Calonita for always being my first, and always enthusiastic, reader. I'm also grateful for Kirk Benshoff for his help with my website. And, of course, my family's continued support of Author Elizabeth means the world to me.

Words could never properly convey how grateful I am to every teacher, librarian, bookseller, and blogger who has talked about Shelby and Watson or placed this book into a child's hand. Authors can't do what we do without readers, so thank you, thank you, THANK YOU!